CHRISTMAS WEDDING

Song

Also by Phyllis Clark Nichols

THE FAMILY PORTRAIT
The Christmas Portrait – Book One
The Birthday Portrait – Book Two

THE ROCKWATER SUITE
Return of the Song – Book One
Freedom of the Song – Book Two
Ransom for a Song – Book Three

Christmas at Grey Sage
Silent Days, Holy Night

CHRISTMAS
WEDDING
Song

The ROCKWATER Suite

—

Book Four

Phyllis Clark Nichols

Southern
Stories
Publishing

CHRISTMAS WEDDING SONG: Book #4 in The Rockwater Suite

Copyright © 2020 by Phyllis Clark Nichols

Published by Southern Stories Publishing

ISBN: 978-1-7344522-6-6 (paperback)
ISBN: 978-1-7344522-7-3 (ebook)
Print Edition

Cover art and design by Bill Nichols and Christy Nichols Quinn

Dedication

For my husband Bill,
who makes every day a celebration of life and love

Chapter 1

Presents and Portents

————————◆————————

Tuesday, December 8, 2009
Moss Point

Caroline was alone on this wintry, early December afternoon, her only company Mozart's "Sleigh Ride from Three German Dances." She barely heard the back doorbell over the recording of the sleigh bells. Balancing her steaming cup of Darjeeling, she dodged the cartons stacked around the kitchen floor. She could see Angel through the kitchen window and hurried to answer. "Come in, Angel. It's freezing out there." She closed the door and guided Angel through the maze of boxes to the great room. "Careful. I'm afraid this place is a mess."

"Oh, get me near that fireplace, girl, before I turn into an eighty-six-year-old human popsicle. I believe it's already the coldest December on record, and we're only a few days into the month." Angel walked slowly across the room and leaned toward the fire to warm her hands, then turned around. "Hope I'm not interrupting, but it looks like I am."

"As always, your timing's perfect." Caroline put her

teacup on the table and moved the box off the chair. "I needed a break. I'm beginning to wonder what possessed me to get married at Christmas. You should have cautioned me about all the wedding details. And then on top of that the Christmas shopping and endless decisions. Yes, I truly need a break. I just made myself a cup of tea, and the water's still hot in the kettle."

"Yes, yes! I'd love a cup, but I suppose the cookie jar's packed." Angel sat down in the chair she'd been sitting in the last seven years whenever she came to the studio to hear Caroline play the piano.

Caroline had moved to the kitchen. "Sorry, you're right," she said as she rummaged for a mug. "Trying to get everything packed up for the movers coming day after tomorrow. But if you care for a cookie, I do have a stash."

"I don't ever recall saying no to one of your cookies."

Caroline poured steaming water over a tea bag and reached for a paper plate. "I made a batch yesterday, so I'd have fresh cookies for Betsy and for myself while I'm still here." She sighed, remembering the sadness that had shrouded her when she realized it was the last tray of cookies she'd take out of this oven. For seven years, her cookie jar had never been empty, always ready to share her sweets with Sam and Angel and her students.

She had the same feeling of nostalgia as she looked at Angel sitting in her favorite chair in front of the fireplace.

In three days, Caroline would be driving to Rockwater, not to return to Twin Oaks as a single woman. There'd be no more afternoons at the piano with Angel and Sam listening to her. This studio, the gardens, and having Sam and Angel just a walk up the hill for the last seven years had given her a sense of peace and security. Now her life was about to change.

She maneuvered her way through the boxes and set the

cup of tea on the table next to Angel. Handing her the plate, she said, "Snickerdoodles with extra cinnamon."

"Mmm, my favorite." Angel looked up at her. "So, tell me, do you suppose Lilah will allow you to make cookies in the kitchen at Rockwater?"

"I may have to negotiate that since she's quite a baker herself, and Roderick has grown up on her cooking." Caroline sat on the hearth, her cup in hand. The fire provided not only warmth but a golden glow in the grayness of what was becoming a somber afternoon. She was glad to see the warmth had put a bit of color back into Angel's cheeks.

"Just offer to sing her a song, and you'll get anything you want."

"Oh, how I wish it could be that simple." She paused, studying Angel's expression. "All this packing has given me so much time to think. My life's really about to change, isn't it?"

"Yes, sweet girl, it is." Angel sipped her tea. "But the good news is this: your address is about to change, but you'll make new friends. Your daily routine won't be the same, but you will be. You will be the same talented, thoughtful, bright girl I've loved for nearly thirty years."

"All those ups and downs, and you still love me?" Caroline smiled in adoration. "You've seen me through every season of my life, especially the last one. You've been like a warm blanket on my coldest days, and yet you gave me all the space I needed to grieve and wrestle with my faith and life and the . . . dailiness of my days. And you gave me this incredible studio, my place to be, my place to heal and put my life back together." Setting down her teacup, she crawled the few feet across the timeworn oak floor to Angel. She rested her head on Angel's knees and wiped her silent tears with the sleeve of her sweater. "I'm going to miss you so much, Angel. And Sam. Who will I call now? All my adult life, I've always called Sam or my dad, and they were only steps away when I needed them."

"You'll still call Sam. He'll be expecting that. And you'll be coming back this way and down to Fernwood to see your parents so often you won't have time to miss us or your family." Angel stroked Caroline's hair. "Remember our conversation last spring after Roderick asked you to marry him? I told you that now you had someplace and someone to go to. That's different than running from something or someone. I'd be sad if I thought your heart only held happiness right now. I'd worry about you if you didn't have some tender feelings about leaving this place and us. You're just having the normal bride's jitters."

"I have no jitters about Roderick, but I am sad to be leaving everything and everyone I love."

"Don't you think Roderick knows that? And that man loves you more than you know. And after nearly losing you in the jungles of Guatemala last summer, he's going to spend every day trying to make you smile. That's what he promised Sam and me the night he walked out of our kitchen door and down to the studio to ask you to marry him." Angel paused. "After all, if the man will fly his plane to Guatemala to rescue you from kidnappers, I imagine he'll fly you anyplace you'd like to go. Your life will be magical because you're marrying your prince."

They sat together quietly as the music ended and the fire crackled. Angel broke the comforting silence. "Betsy's coming in later this evening?"

"Around eight thirty. She won't leave Fernwood until Mason gets home to take care of the kids, and then she'll return home tomorrow afternoon."

"That's a best friend for you. Driving all this way just to spend one more night with you here in the studio."

"Since childhood, we've had our spend-the-night parties, and they haven't stopped. Oh, and all those nights she spent with me after David was killed."

The room fell quiet again as they both pondered those days. The shock of David's death in a mudslide in Guatemala six weeks before their wedding had changed the trajectory of Caroline's life. And it had been another mudslide in the Guatemala Highlands just months ago that saved her from kidnappers during her trip to launch the Guatemalan children's choir. She rubbed the shoulder that had been broken in that near disaster.

"Your shoulder still giving you trouble?"

"Oh, it's healed, but I think this cold, damp weather and all this packing have angered my bones."

Angel took her last sip of tea and brushed the cookie crumbs from her sweater. "Nothing that some rest and a honeymoon in the tropics won't cure. I'd best get myself up and get back to the house. And before I forget what I came for . . ." She reached into her pocket sweater and pulled out a velvet bag and handed it to Caroline. "Remember these?"

Caroline gently poured the bag's contents into her hand. "Your pink sapphires?"

"Yes, and I want you to have them. You dazzled Roderick Adair in that pink gown and these sapphires on your first trip to Rockwater to play your recital. They belong to you now."

"But, Angel . . ."

"No buts. I know Roderick can buy you anything you want, but he cannot buy you these. Consider them an early Christmas present."

"Thank you, Angel. I will treasure them always." They stood and embraced, clinging to each other and to the string of memories that would always bind them.

"Enough of this mushy, moping around stuff. I also

came to tell we're having beef stew and cornbread at five thirty, and I expect to see you at the table."

Angel headed through the kitchen and out the door. Caroline watched her walk the path and take the turn to the mailbox. Then she opened her palm to look again at the pink sapphires and remembered a night at Rockwater.

———•———

Sam ambled from his study to the kitchen. "You two sound like a couple of magpies fussing over a worm in here." He propped his cane on the back of his chair and sat down at the breakfast table.

Hattie stood at the back door, buttoning her coat. "I done made the corn bread, and the beef stew's been simmerin' all afternoon. But you know Miss Angel. She ain't happy 'less she's doin' somethin', so she's makin' a salad. I tol' her nobody wants a green salad when it's as cold as an outhouse on a January night. They want somethin' bone-stickin' warm." She put on her gloves and waved. "I'll be back tomorrow. Y'all enjoy that cold salad now."

Angel opened the refrigerator to retrieve the lettuce and a jar of mayonnaise. "Oh, nobody will eat the lettuce. It's just for presentation. And you be careful on the roads, Hattie."

Sam chimed in. "Angel's right. Roads could be wet, and it's freezing out there. See you in the morning." With a final wave as Hattie went out the door, he slid the stack of mail to where he could sort it. "I see you picked up the mail." He looked inquiringly at Angel. "How was your visit with Caroline?"

"Just so you know, I'm not making a tossed salad. I'm just putting some lettuce under the canned pears. And my visit with Caroline was . . . Well, it was parsimonious." Angel opened the jar of mayonnaise and spooned some into each pear half.

"Another one of Ned's new words?" Sam smiled, thinking of Ned and Fred, the sixty-five-year-old twins that helped them around Twin Oaks. Fred rarely opened his mouth, so Ned spoke for both of them, and lately, fifty-cent words had filled his new vocabulary.

"Yep. Ned keeps me turning the pages of my dictionary. It means 'frugal and restrained,' not like this cheddar cheese." She sprinkled a heavy layer of shredded cheese on top of the pears.

Sam began sorting envelopes. "Did you give her the sapphires like you planned? Nothing frugal or restrained about that."

Angel put the platter of pears on the table and held on to the back of the chair. "I did, and she loved them. But we were more frugal and restrained with our emotions. Seeing that studio filled with boxes that'll be leaving Twin Oaks on Friday pulled at my heartstrings. And I know there was more than boxes pulling on hers. Neither of us would let loose, or I'm telling you we would have needed the mop for the tears. The reality of the big changes coming are beginning to settle in and get more real to her." Angel pulled out her chair and sat for a brief rest.

Sam looked up from sorting Christmas cards and junk mail. "She's a smart girl. She's been thinking and examining all of this for months now. She'll adjust just like she did when she moved here after David was killed."

"That's what I told her. She's just feeling the pain of last things. Even in her joy and anticipation, there's a bit of grief." Angel stood, picked up the stack of junk mail and headed for the trash can under the sink.

"And she's had enough of that. We knew when she

came here it was temporary, and it did last longer than I thought it would. You know how that girl is about goodbyes."

Caroline's acceptance of their invitation to live in the studio after David's death had thrilled Sam. The families had been friends for years, and he and Angel had become her surrogate parents. Having her living at Twin Oaks and teaching piano to the town's children had been like having the daughter they always wanted. Her music was an added gift.

Angel went to the cabinet to get out the bowls and plates. "She's about to say hello to a whole new world. Who would have ever guessed that when she started searching for her childhood piano last year, she would find her piano and John Roderick Adair?"

"And don't forget Rockwater, that Kentucky estate of his."

Angel turned with raised eyebrows. "Who could forget that? And she'll be getting married there in just two weeks. I know it'll be her new home, but I still wish she was getting married here."

"Yes, and her mother's probably saying the same thing, wishing she was getting married in Fernwood. You know Caroline. She's just not into all that fuss. She wants something meaningful and real." Sam began opening the Christmas cards, since Angel had already tossed what he called "letter litter." "You know, with the wedding coming up and then Christmas, we need to go through these year-end requests and decide how much we're giving away this year before time gets away from us." He skimmed and stacked the requests until he came to a letter in an ivory linen envelope with no stamp or return address. The way it was addressed to the both of them gave the appearance of a personal letter. He turned it over to see if there was a seal or return address on the back side. Nothing. "Well, this is odd—a letter with no stamp, postmark, or return address."

"It's Christmas. Maybe it's from Santa. Just read it and see if we've been bad or good." Angel carefully took the hot iron skillet of cornbread out of the oven.

"Maybe Santa doesn't know it's a federal offense to put something like this in a residential mailbox." Sam took out the pocketknife he'd carried since he was a boy and turned the envelope over. The razor-sharp blade slid through the linen paper as easily as the butter that would melt on Angel's warm cornbread. He unfolded the linen stationery and looked down the page for a signature. There was none. He quickly scanned the one paragraph.

Dear Mr. and Mrs. Meadows,

I write this as a last resort. I'm warning you that you're about to let Caroline Carlyle make the most serious mistake of her life. I know she is planning to wed Roderick Adair, and her time is running out. You are responsible for what happens if she marries him. Unless she wants her heart and her life broken into little pieces and scattered over the Kentucky bluegrass, she will think twice. Do your best to keep her from marrying him so that I don't have to intervene. You will be sorry.

Sam leaned back in his chair, stunned and puzzled. He read the paragraph again more slowly before calling Angel. "Come read this. I'm not sure what to make of it."

"So, Santa's giving us a warning to be good?"

"Somebody's giving us a warning for sure."

Angel dried her hands, walked to the table, and picked up the letter. Sam studied the growing discomfort on her face as her eyes moved down the page. When she finished, she waved the letter in the air. "What? What is this? I don't know what to make of this either." She threw the letter on the table and looked into Sam's eyes. "Should we be worried?"

His brow was creased with apprehension, but he tried to hide it. "What, about this? Oh, I don't think so. I've never been one to put much stock in anything that somebody won't sign. Anonymous won't cut it with me."

Angel sat down. "But that last sentence . . . 'So that I don't have to intervene.' That sounds like a threat to me."

Before Sam could respond, he heard the back-porch door slam. "It's Caroline." He folded the letter and stuck it into the stack of mail and handed the stack to Angel. "Don't say anything to Caroline. She doesn't need to be thinking about this right now."

Chapter 2

A Letter and a Package

———◆———

Tuesday night, December 8
Moss Point

Caroline stacked the last of the firewood on the smoldering embers. Perhaps this wouldn't be the last time she warmed her feet in front of this fireplace, she decided. Sam had suggested in dinner table conversation that she and Roderick could use the studio as their own guest cottage when they came to visit. She'd noticed how excited Angel became with talk of buying new furnishings for the studio so that she and Roderick would be comfortable. Somehow knowing Angel would fix up the studio for their visits made leaving feel less final. And it wouldn't be the last bowl of beef stew and Hattie's cornbread.

She grabbed her wedding notebook and a pencil. Settled on the sofa with a blanket, she dialed Roderick's number.

His baritone voice still made her pulse flicker like butterfly wings. "Hello, this is Roderick Adair. Leave your name and number, and I'll get back to you. But for now, I'm preparing myself and Rockwater for a wedding. I have waited my whole life for my bride, the love of my life, and as of today, I only must wait one more week and four days. The Georgia parties are over, and just one more event in Lexington. Then the wedding, and finally I'll have her all to myself. So maybe I won't have time to call you back, but please leave a message anyway."

She sat quietly twirling her black curls around her finger while a broad smile seeped across her face. "So, you looked at your caller ID?"

"Hello, this is Roderick Adair. Leave your—" He laughed.

She warmed to his chuckle. "Your bride is one blessed woman to have such a man counting the days, and the word is she's happier than you are that the parties are over."

"Not much of a party girl, is she?"

She tucked the blanket under her feet. "Nope, never was. She prefers quiet evenings and sweet music and someone to hold her hand. Know where she might find someone who would share her preferences?"

"I believe I do. He's waiting for her at Rockwater."

"Then she'll be there Friday by five o'clock." His gravelly chuckle put a smile on her face.

"I'm not just counting days. I'm counting hours. You are making me the happiest man on the planet, Caroline Carlyle. I never dared to dream you could love me enough to marry me."

"If I can make it through the next several days and all the details, the planet will have two deliriously happy people walking around on it." She doodled on the clean sheet of her wedding notebook.

"Glad to hear that. Sorry to add to the decisions, but there are two immediate issues we haven't settled yet. First, what about your piano? I know we'll be bringing your Hazelton Brothers piano back to Rockwater—something

I'm very glad about since this is the piano that brought us together. But what do you want to do with your grand piano that is sitting here, the one I traded you?"

The remembrance of playing her childhood piano again at her Rockwater recital made her happy, and especially the memory of walking into her studio a few weeks after the recital and finding Roderick and her Hazelton Brothers piano sitting there together. He had made the swap so that she could have her choice, but now it would be their piano. "Of course I want our piano brought back to Rockwater, and what would you think about giving my grand to Bella? I asked my parents if they'd like to have it, and they don't. I thought of leaving it here so that I could play when we visit Sam and Angel, but that seems such a waste. Pianos are meant to be played, and I really love the idea that Bella is playing it." She made herself a note.

"That's a beautiful thought, Caroline, just like you. Have you talked to Gretchen? You know this is a grand piano, and they're in a small cottage. Is there room?"

"Yes. She said she would make room and the arrangements to get it there."

"No need for that. When the movers deliver your piano here, I'll have them deliver this one to Durham right after Christmas. That means they'll both be here for several days."

"Gretchen and Bella will be at the wedding, and I'll do something special so that Bella will know it's our Christmas present to her. That's done, so what's next?"

"It's about Friday and your driving yourself up here."

She sat up a bit straighter at the thought. "We've already talked about that one, and the decision is made."

"It seems *you* made the decision, but *we* didn't. Now hear me out. The weather's not great, and neither is your car. That's an eight- or nine-hour drive. Humor me so that I won't worry. Why not just leave the car in Moss Point? Acer and I will fly down and get you."

"But I'll need my car."

"No, you'll need *a* car, and we'll get you one. I know you love your car, but it has seen its better days, Caroline. Maybe Sam could sell it for you or just leave it there for us to use when we visit." He paused. "Will you please think about it? I really don't like you driving alone that distance."

Caroline tapped her pencil against her lip for a moment before gusting out a sigh. "You win. You and Acer come get me and leave room in the plane for all the stuff I was bringing in my car. Things like my wedding dress and the sentimental things I just couldn't pack for the movers to carry."

"We'll leave plenty of room in the cargo area, and I'll get Acer to file the flight plan first thing in the morning. We'll be there by eleven on Friday." She noted the tension in his voice had disappeared. "Suppose we could get Hattie to fry some chicken for lunch?"

Caroline heard the doorbell. She looked at the clock on the table. Eight forty. "I think Betsy's here. I'll call you later around bedtime."

"Good. I have news about the master suite. It's almost finished, and it has your touch—your beautiful, warm touch."

"I can't wait to hear every detail, and I'll check on the fried chicken for Friday lunch." She unwrapped herself and put her notebook and pencil on the bar as she walked to the door. "Love you and later."

"Love you and always."

Caroline opened the terrace door. Betsy, a good head taller than Caroline, lumbered through with a tote bag hanging on her shoulder, pulling a red bag on wheels and balancing a small box in her free hand. "My goodness, it's cold. The temperature dropped when the sun went down, and it was already frigid."

Caroline took the box from her hand. "I'm so glad you're here. Can you believe it? Our last night in the studio because I'm getting married. Still sounds strange coming out of my mouth. 'I'm getting married and moving to Rockwater.'"

Betsy balanced her red bag and dropped her tote bag from her shoulder to the floor beside her luggage. She hugged Caroline. "I know. I know you're getting married. Finally. I prayed so long that God would bring you someone who loved you, and wow, did He ever answer my prayer." She took off her coat and draped it over the barstool. "Roderick loves you, he's handsome, he's kind, and he's wealthy. And more than anything, he wants to make you happy. I guess all that was worth waiting for God to provide."

Caroline was on the way around the counter to the kitchen. "Yes, Roderick is worth the wait. Not in my boldest dreams would I have imagined, let alone ask God for, someone like Roderick." She went around the corner, setting down Betsy's package as she did. "Tea? And I have cookies."

"Yes, chamomile unless you've packed it."

Caroline reached for the tea kettle and turned on the stove. "Most everything is packed except the last-minute stuff."

"But that's why I came, to help you pack." Betsy moved her jacket and sat on the barstool, peering over the bar into the kitchen as Caroline rummaged for the tea bags. "Looks like you've been busy. How did you decide what to pack? He has everything in the world at Rockwater. What do you have here that he doesn't already have two of? You were smart not to request wedding gifts."

"I did so request wedding gifts, just not for us but for

the Guatemalan Children's Choir. And besides, I have some favorite things here in the kitchen that I want to take with me. I'm not planning to give up cooking just because Roderick has Lilah. That is if she'll allow me, and I think she will. We've cooked together before." She pushed the box of cookies over to Betsy.

"Lilah. Do you know what I'd give for a Lilah? Someone who managed the household so that I could spend all my time with Josefina and little David, who just happens to be getting into all creation now."

"Already." Shaking her head, Caroline readied two teacups.

Betsy dropped her car keys into her bag on the floor. "Yep. He's into everything not nailed down, just like his daddy."

"What about Josefina? She's probably a big help."

"Well, she was until she got into this flower-girl phase. She is more excited about being your flower-girl than about what Santa will be bringing her for Christmas. Can't wait for you to see her. She's been prancing around balancing a book on her head practicing her wedding walk for weeks now."

Caroline smiled at the thought. She had been with Betsy and Mason when they all but gave up on having children of their own. She had prayed for them. She had made the trip with them to Guatemala when they adopted Josefina four years ago. And then, after all the waiting, little David had appeared. Not only was the pregnancy a surprise, but the doctor had told them they were having a girl. So this little person had shocked them all, and with Caroline's permission, they'd named him David. Mason and David had been best friends in college, and he had introduced David to her. Now they were celebrating her marriage to Roderick, and Josefina would be her flower girl.

Caroline leaned forward and propped her elbows on the kitchen counter and looked at Betsy. "God's just full of surprises—Josefina, little David, and now Roderick. But I was telling Angel today that I really messed things up planning a Christmas wedding. It's almost too much for everyone."

Betsy sighed. "I tried to tell you, but I think it's beautiful. You are getting to do things your way. Your mom even got to have her big shindig down in Ferngrove. By the way, people are still talking about that. Your folks really outdid themselves to celebrate you and Roderick. And now the wedding will be the one of your dreams—not your mother's dream or Angel's dream, but yours."

Caroline reached for the teakettle and poured steaming water into the waiting cups. "I don't mean to sound ungrateful, but I'm so glad the big parties are almost over. Roderick has been introduced to all my relatives and all the citizens of Ferngrove and Moss Point. Sarah's hosting one more small gathering to introduce me to his close friends and business associates, then we get to have the quiet wedding each of us wants. We'll be surrounded by the people we love, and it will be simple and perfect, not like some of the fiascos I've played for through the years."

Caroline set the timer for four minutes. "While the tea steeps, I need to give Angel a quick call before she goes to bed. Roderick wants fried chicken. I'll explain later."

Caroline dialed the Meadows' number. Sam answered. "Hi, Sam. It's the piano player down the hill. Has Angel gone to bed?"

"She's sitting in her chair in front of the fire knitting away. Would you like to speak with her?"

"Maybe you could just ask her. We've had a change in plans. Roderick and Acer are flying in to pick me up on Friday. He really doesn't like the idea of my driving to

Lexington in my old car. So he was wondering if Hattie might fry some chicken and we could all have lunch together."

"Don't need to disturb Angel for that. I'll fry the chicken myself if it means you won't be making that trip alone and we get to have lunch with you and Roderick. Tell him yes."

She imagined Sam sitting tall in his chair with a big smile, knowing he could deliver that message to Angel. "Great. Betsy and I'll see you in the morning."

"Glad you're coming for breakfast. That means I get pancakes."

She giggled. "Sam, you get pancakes anytime you want them. You'd better not let Angel hear you talking like that."

"Yep. I've already gotten the eye. You know the one. Good night, my sweet girl."

———•———

Sam put the phone down. "Well, there's been a change in plans."

Angel kept knitting. "I gathered that. Sounds like Roderick's coming Friday. What's going on?"

Sam rubbed his chin. "Caroline said he didn't want her driving all that distance by herself, so he's flying down to get her."

"I think that's a fabulous idea. I was worried about that old rattletrap she drives, and that's a long way from here to Lexington." She rolled the extra thread around the ball of yarn and put her knitting away in the basket next to her chair.

"Well, it hasn't been that long since he rescued her in Guatemala, and he's not wanting to take any chances.

Besides, it's a long way to Lexington in many ways, and this change of plans is good. It means Roderick's looking out for her, and it means I get a chance to talk to him about this letter we received. And it won't be over the phone. I can look him in the eye when I tell him."

"But I thought you were going to file that with the letter litter and forget about it."

He took off his glasses and rubbed his eyes. "I thought I was, but I can't seem to let it go. If whoever sent this letter had just not written that last sentence, I think I could have. But that threat rattles my gut instincts a bit. The same kind of feeling I had when we didn't know who was snooping around down at the studio, and then we learned it was Bella. These kinds of things don't always turn out with such a happy ending. I don't want some unhinged crazy woman messing up Caroline's wedding."

Angel moved to the front of her chair. "An unhinged crazy woman, is it? So, you've figured this out. You think it's a woman?"

"Gotta be. Men don't write letters like that. Now, I don't believe a word of it, but it's seems to me it's the act of a jealous woman, and she must be a bit unhinged not to know what she did is against the law and to be making up lies like that, and then threatening to stop this marriage. Whoever she is, well, she doesn't know old Sam."

"Well, your theory sounds reasonable, and unhinged seems unpredictable to me."

"That's the truth, and we don't need unpredictability. I'll just have a man-to-man conversation with Roderick and put him on alert. And by the way, he wants fried chicken for lunch on Friday."

Angel rose from her chair and went to the fireplace. "That can be arranged, but right now *this* unhinged woman is going to bed. I'll think about all this tomorrow. And we're still not mentioning this to Caroline, right?"

"Right."

Angel walked toward the hallway. "Don't stay up to late."

Sam stared into the flames. "I'll be there shortly. I'll make certain the fire is out." He sat quietly pondering. *Caroline doesn't need to know anything about this. I don't want it spoiling this girl's happiness. Hopefully, it's nothing to worry about, but it's best to tell Roderick and put this fire out, too, before it catches and destroys something beautiful.*

———•———

Betsy settled on her customary end of the sofa with her cup of tea. "Speaking of wedding presents, aren't you going to open the package I brought in? Looks like a present."

Caroline looked at the box on the counter. "Oh, is the package for me? I just thought it was something you brought with you."

"Nope. It's not from me. It was on the rug at the terrace door. I figured you weren't here when it was delivered. Didn't you say you went up to have dinner with Sam and Angel?"

"I did, and the package wasn't here when I left." She lifted the box and looked at it. Only her name typed on a white sheet of paper and taped onto the box. No shipping label. No barcode. No return address. She shook it. No rattle. "Whatever it is, it's light, and it wasn't delivered like other packages." She went to her desk for the letter opener and slid it through the tape.

"Probably someone in town who just couldn't resist giving you a proper wedding present and wanted to see you one more time before you leave." Betsy cozied herself under the blanket and stretched her legs, which almost reached the other end of the sofa.

Caroline opened the flaps of the box lid, revealing a bold-typed note.

This is a warning. If you marry Roderick Adair, this will be your future.

"What? Is this a joke?" She removed the note and unfolded the tissue paper. A red-satin, heart-shaped pillow had been ripped in half, and the batting was strewn around the interior of the box. She gasped.

Betsy turned to her. "Wow. Sounds like a nice gift."

Stunned and puzzled, Caroline said nothing but stared into the box.

"Caroline, what's in the package?"

Unable to speak, Caroline turned to see Betsy tossing the blanket from her legs, getting up from the sofa, and walking to the desk where Caroline stood frozen. Caroline handed her the note.

"What?" Betsy put the note on the desk and snatched the box from Caroline. She glared at the desecrated red pillow. "This is mean. Just plain mean."

Caroline began to shake as a chill ran through her body. Seeing this, Betsy tossed the box to the floor and hugged her, soothing her the way she had the night Caroline learned David had been killed.

That thought pulled a sob from Caroline. "Just when everything seemed so perfect." She pulled away to look at Betsy. "Am I just not meant to be happy, Betsy?"

Chapter 3

No Secrets

———— ◆ ————

Wednesday, December 9
Rockwater

*R*oderick eyed the trees framing the piano and then looked at Lilah. "Do you think it might be a bit early to have the Christmas trees delivered and decorated? It's ten days before the wedding."

Lilah stood with a box of silver balls in one hand and the other hand on her hip. "I've been taking care of you and Rockwater for nearly forty years now, and if I thought that, I wouldn't be decorating them, would I? It's just over a week before the wedding, and there's much to do. Besides, Fletcher says the trees are guaranteed. They weren't cut. You do see they're in huge pots. Caroline wants to plant them on the property when the ground thaws in the spring. Fletcher will help us take care of that too."

"Oh, she didn't tell me that, but I like the idea." Roderick took the box of ornaments from Lilah and followed her around the tree.

"That girl's full of surprises, and she thinks you're busy

and didn't want to bother you with those kinds of details. She and I are working on all this, getting the house decorated for Christmas and for the wedding. And, I might add, Caroline wants nothing, and I mean nothing, extra for the wedding. She thinks the house is so beautiful at Christmas that there's no need for wedding decorations. Simply elegant is what she is and what she wants."

"I think I still own this manor, and there will be one extra thing for the wedding. Could you get the florist to deliver a big bouquet of white irises for the master suite?"

"Oh, yes. I'll be happy to take care of that. Did you tell her about the suite?" Lilah continued hanging the silver balls on the perfectly shaped Douglas fir.

Roderick handed her another ornament. "No, not yet. Betsy arrived while we were talking last night. She came up to spend their last night together before the wedding. Their version of a bachelorette party, I suppose. Caroline gave me a quick call before bedtime, and there was no time to give her the details."

"Speaking of bachelorette party, are you to have a bachelor's party?"

Roderick laughed. "Not planning on it. I think I've aged out of bachelor parties. Besides, I'm taking my cue from Caroline and keeping things simple. I may take her dad and brothers hunting the day before the wedding, but that's to get out of the house so you ladies can have a good time." He looked at the four Douglas firs, one large one and one smaller one on each side of the grand piano. "You do realize this piano, the one with the trees you're decorating all around it, will have another one sitting beside it when the movers arrive on Friday?"

"No, but I figured as much. But I'll be here with my broom to make sure they don't touch one of these trees. So, tell, me, what happens to this piano?"

"For a few days, it will be here."

"That's a treat. We have two pianists; we might as well have two grand pianos. It's Christmas, and you can never have too much music at Christmas."

"But just for Christmas. Earlier this morning, I arranged for the movers to pick this one up and deliver it to Gretchen and Bella down in Durham after Christmas. Caroline wants Bella to have it." Roderick watched the smile spread across Lilah's caramel-colored face.

Lilah paused from hanging the ornaments to look at Roderick. "That's just like our new Mrs. Adair. She's so much like your mother, Roderick. A giver, that girl. She loves music, flowers, simple things, and you. I like to think your parents are walking around together in heaven, holding hands and smiling inside and out about all of this. And Miss Angeleah? She just might have had a little something to do with it. I'm thinking she had her own conversation with the good Lord on your behalf."

"Mother was always hard to say no to, and I'm not sure even God could quieten her if something was on her mind."

Lilah twirled the bell-shaped ornament in her hand. "Think about it, and you'll agree. After your father died, you got rid of your mother's piano because there was no one to play it, and you built yourself a cottage out back so you didn't have to live in this house alone." Lilah pointed to the windows where Roderick's cottage sat in view under the oak tree. "Then later, you couldn't bear it that this space right here was empty, so you searched until you found a piano that looked just like your mother's and you bought it." She stopped talking and looked back at him. "Now what's the chance of that piano belonging to a young woman who is absolutely perfect for you and who just happened to be searching for her childhood piano? I'd say that has Miss Angeleah's fingerprints all over it."

Roderick hugged Lilah. "Never thought about it quite like that. But it's true. Mother and Father would have loved Caroline. Sarah certainly loves her like a sister. And I do hope they approve of what we've decided to do with their master suite."

Lilah pulled away from him. "I don't want to hear any more talk of *their* suite. They're living in their heavenly mansion, and this is your house now. Your parents left it to you. And you and Caroline are making it every bit your own, and it will be filled with music and flowers and life again, just like your parents wanted." She hung the bell on the tree so that it sparkled in the afternoon sun.

"Day after tomorrow, Caroline will be here, home. Acer and I are flying to get her."

Lilah winked at him. "The suite will be finished by the time you get back on Friday."

"Not an issue. She has her own plans about that too. I'll be staying in my apartment, and she'll stay in one of the guest suites because she wants our wedding night to be the first night in the new master suite."

"What? You still haven't been able to talk her into a honeymoon?"

"Yes and no. She wants to stay here for Christmas and New Year's. Maybe I can surprise her with a quick visit to her parents on Christmas day and Sam and Angel the day after."

"You are one blessed man. I remember some of those women you dated, the ones who would have sacrificed their own mamas to marry you. You can be assured there would have been no simple wedding. We're talking a ceremony in the largest church to be found south of the Mason-Dixon Line, walking the aisle in a designer gown to get that ring on her finger. Then she'd be on her way to the reception at the largest hotel within driving distance, and a honeymoon on a yacht with a full staff. Not Caroline. She's real, Roderick, real. And she knows what matters."

Roderick shook his finger in Lilah's face. "Don't forget. It matters to her that she gets to do some of the Christmas decorating and some cooking, so slow down a bit, and leave something for her to do." He put the box of ornaments on the piano. "And for your information, there will be a honeymoon in the tropics after Christmas. So you'll get some rest while we're gone. You'll need it after a Christmas wedding."

Lilah stacked the half-empty ornament box in the bin on the floor. "Okay. I'll stop for now. But there'll be plenty for Caroline to do around here. We're putting trees in every room just like we did last year when she came to play the recital. You remember, it was that Kentucky moon that shined its light on you two last Christmas. That old moon cast its spell and gave you the courage to tell her you loved her. And this Christmas, you're about to make her your wife."

"The moon will be full on New Year's this year." Roderick kissed Lilah's warm cheek and looked at his watch. "Gotta run. I need to make a couple of business calls before it's too late to call London." He walked down the hallway lined with glass, enjoying the view of the seemingly endless acres of Rockwater.

Lilah mumbled to herself. "Um-huh. I hear you. Seems like the sun never sets on Adair Enterprises. Business is like evil. It just never sleeps. Go take care of your business because your business is about to change, my boy."

"I heard that." Roderick kept walking, but smiled, knowing that what Lilah said was true. Everything was changing—and for the better.

Christmas Wedding Song

—◆—

Ferngrove

Martha penciled her notes on her calendar and turned to her husband, J., seated at the breakfast table next to her. "All set. Just got off the phone with Caroline."

"I heard your side of that conversation and bits and pieces of what CC said, and I want you to know I'm proud of you for not mentioning again your disappointment that the wedding won't be in Ferngrove. That song has been sung quite enough. So, what's all set?"

"Don't tell me what song not to sing. Our only daughter, and she doesn't want a big wedding in her home church? That just doesn't sit well with me." With a pointed look, she turned and made note of something else she'd just remembered.

"That's Caroline, and it's her wedding. She did agree to wear your wedding dress, and you did throw a party bigger than a wedding to introduce Roderick to all our friends."

She was glad J. couldn't see the frown on her face. "Yes, but there was no shower tea, no gifts, and I don't even know if I'll recognize my wedding dress. She's had it altered and probably remade."

J. adjusted his glasses and stretched to look at her calendar. "Can't you just be happy? Our girl is marrying a man who loves her and who will take such good care of her. And look what God brought them through to bring them together. That's a lot to thank the good Lord for, Martha."

"Yes, and I am thankful. But . . ." She couldn't help the bit of self-pity rearing its ugly head. "I just had other expectations. And I thought she'd come home and spend some time before she goes to Rockwater, but she's not." Her mother's heart ached.

"Well, you might remember she has been spending a lot of time with us over the last few months, all the parties and recuperating from her injuries in Guatemala. J. continued looking at the calendar. "Can't make out your writing there. So, what is it that's all set?"

"A couple of things. Roderick is sending the plane Friday for Caroline."

J. slapped the table with open palms. "Yes. I'm glad for that. She didn't have any business trying to make that trip in her car."

"Well, looks like we won't have to make the trip in our car either. She and Roderick want us to drive up to Moss Point on Wednesday the eighteenth, and the two of them will fly down and pick up Sam and Angel and us. He wants us to be there for a small gathering of some of his friends on Wednesday evening. Then they'd like us to spend a couple of days with them before the wedding. We'll leave our car at Sam and Angel's, and the four of us will be flown back to Twin Oaks after the wedding on Saturday afternoon."

"And you're grumbling because Caroline's not coming home?" Her husband's eyes twinkled. "They've invited us all up to see them, and we don't have to make that long drive up and back for the wedding. Don't know how it could get better than that."

Martha reached for the box at the end of the table and pulled out a stack of envelopes and Christmas cards. "But that means we won't be driving up for the wedding with the boys and their families. James rented a twelve-passenger van so we could all go together, and he could probably have rented one for eight passengers if we had only known."

"You mean we'll be missing out on eight hours of riding with nonstop-yapping adults and three rambunctious children? I love 'em, but I say 'Whoopee.' And they'll need the van for all that luggage and Christmas presents." He paused. "Is that all you're worried about?

"Nope. She didn't come to her senses about the honeymoon or the holidays either. They'll be staying at Rockwater. They're not even coming home for Christmas . . ." She trailed off, knowing how childish she sounded.

J. shook his head and stood up. "Martha, I'm headed to the workshop, and while I'm out there, maybe you should have a little talk with yourself and see if you can get out from under that gray cloud you've let settle all around you. There's a big blue sky of good things happening. We have two sons and their families who live around the corner. And they'll all be here for Christmas. Besides, we're having our family Christmas the night before the wedding, and we'll all be together. Be happy about that, and forget about your expectations."

Martha bit her lip as though it might keep her tongue from moving, but it didn't. "I know, but it's at Rockwater. That's not Christmas. It just doesn't seem right."

"Martha, give those two a break. Caroline met Roderick a year and a half ago, and they've lived hours apart, trying to get to know each other long distance between crises. Do you remember all that's happened in that year?" He ticked off his list on his fingers. "Caroline met Bella and Gretchen and took on the responsibility of getting them free of Ernesto and getting them to Duke where they have a chance at a decent life. And then last summer with the kidnapping in Guatemala, when we thought we'd lost her. But through all that, Roderick was there, helping her and rescuing her. And they've had so little time just the two of them. Anytime they've been together has always been with family or Gretchen and Bella."

J. put his hand on Martha's shoulder. "I've never known you to be a selfish woman," he said softly. "They have lives, you know, and their lives should not be expected to revolve around your expectations."

Martha sighed and shook her head before she stood and embraced her husband. "I know. I *know*. *I do* sound ungrateful, don't I? We prayed for years for Caroline to find love again. And honestly, I thought that prayer might never be answered. But she's in such a blessed place right now with Roderick, and she has the hopes of a beautiful future." She nodded firmly. "You're right. Blue skies. Only blue skies and star-filled Christmas nights."

J. squeezed her and kissed her cheek. "That's my Martha. Finish your Christmas cards. I'll be in the shop working on my project."

———•———

Moss Point

Betsy rolled her suitcase into the room, plopped down on the sofa, and looked at her watch. "Okay, CC. I have a few more minutes before I need to get on the road. Anything else I can help you with?"

Caroline wiped the counter. "No, we're done. Everything's packed that should be packed, and the movers will be here tomorrow morning bright and early."

Betsy looked in her bag for her keys. "You want to look down your list one more time? Seems to me I'm getting off easy with this maid-of-honor thing. No bridesmaid's luncheon. No big shower. No helping you keep up with the wedding-gift list. You're wearing your mom's wedding dress, and I got to pick out my own dress. No helping you pick out your honeymoon wardrobe. No tastings for the wedding cake or reception." She laid her keys on the sofa and patted the seat next to her.

Caroline sat down beside her and leaned her head on

Betsy's shoulder. "You're doing what's most important. You're standing with me like you have since kindergarten."

Betsy wanted nothing of a somber, teary farewell. She had a long drive home, and she preferred happier thoughts. She coiled Caroline's curls around her finger. "Your hair's a mess, you know. You want me to try to do something with it before I leave?"

"No, just sit with me. You're the best. I don't know what I would have done without you my whole life. And now that my life is about to change, I want you to know I still need you."

Betsy realized she wouldn't be leaving without some tears after all. "Of course you need me. Who's going to fix this curly mop of yours for your wedding if I'm not around?"

"Cut it out, Betsy. I'm trying to be serious here."

"I know, and it's killing me. You're just not used to these fluctuating emotions. You've been in mourning for David and living in a continual state of beige or maybe gray for years. And finally, after all this time, Roderick steps through the door of your heart, and you're afraid to feel real joy and happiness again. One minute you're excited about marrying him . . . "

". . . And the next minute I'm afraid. I fear I've grown quite comfortable here. Or even worse now after getting that package, I'm afraid something will happen to stop the wedding."

Betsy sat up straight. "I think what you're really afraid of is losing Roderick like you lost David. Life's about risks, CC. Having faith is a risk. Have faith that Roderick is God's gift to you. Risk loving him and giving yourself to all that's coming your way. And that's all I have to say about that." Betsy stood up.

Caroline stood as well and faced her. "I know deep

down it's right. I love Roderick, and I'm certain he loves me. I'm just feeling a little sad, but it's a beautiful sadness."

"I'll have to think about that one. I think the mysterious package spooked you. Forget about it. It's probably someone around here who has a secret crush on you and doesn't want you to leave Moss Point. And when you tell Roderick about it . . ." She saw a slight tightening in Caroline's lips.

"Oh, I wasn't planning on telling Roderick about the package."

Betsy wasn't about to let that one go by. "Then you need to change your plans, CC. No secrets between a wife and her husband. None. Tell him, and just get on that plane Friday and fly away with your love to your new life."

"You're right. The package spooked me a bit, but it's in the garbage where it belongs. And thanks for keeping it quiet from Sam and Angel this morning. No need in stirring up things, and I will tell Roderick. You're right, no secrets."

Chapter 4

Moving Day

———◆———

Thursday, December 10
Moss Point

Caroline woke to another frigid morning, but she was grateful for the blue skies and sunshine that had pushed into oblivion the grayness of the last few days. She rose early and readied herself for the day. She hoped the fair weather meant fairer days ahead.

The studio was as busy as the day before a recital. Only Ned and Fred weren't hauling chairs in and arranging them, and she wasn't in the kitchen baking cookies for her students and their families.

It was moving day. The movers, dressed in khaki pants and red shirts, arrived in a bright-yellow van. Happy colors to go with a startling blue sky. Caroline walked the three of them through the studio and gave instructions.

Larry, the one with the clipboard, asked, "Ma'am, you mean you're not taking everything in here?"

"No, just the boxes that are packed and the few pieces of furniture with the pink sticky notes on them. And the piano of course." Caroline had marked her favorite chair that had been her grandmother's, the chair that had hugged her for years. And she wanted her marble-topped desk and the chifforobe she had used for extra closet space. She had no idea where she might put these things at Rockwater, but they'd be with her. Certainly in a sprawling estate home, she would have places from which to choose.

"Yes, ma'am. We'll make short order of this."

"The only thing I didn't pack is the mantle clock on the desk. My father made it, and I really didn't have a box that was secure enough for it. I was hoping you might have something to keep it safe and undamaged." Caroline had used that clock to time her student's lessons. She had listened to its soft chimes in the middle of the night when she couldn't sleep. She had stared at it wishing time would pass, hoping her days and nights would soon grow brighter. Now her days were happier, and she knew exactly where the clock would find its home. It would sit on the mantle over the fireplace in the newly renovated master suite.

"Yes, ma'am. I'll care for it as if it were my firstborn."

"Thank you, Larry."

"You're welcome. Since it's such a sunshiny day, we'll get all the boxes cleared out and the few pieces of furniture wrapped and stacked on the terrace. That will give us more room to disassemble the piano."

"Disassemble the piano" stunned her. She knew it had to be done, but somehow the thought startled her. The next time she played this piano would be at Rockwater. There would be no more piano playing in this room.

"Miss Carlyle."

"I'm sorry, just the memories surfacing, and the reality that there'll be no more music in this room."

"But there'll be so much music in this instrument's new home. I was just saying that after everything is loaded, we'll do a final walk-through to make certain we've done our job. Then we'll be on our way, and since the weather is fair, we might even make it to Lexington tonight."

"That sounds good." She looked at the piano. "If you don't mind, I'll stay out of your way and play the piano while you're moving boxes."

"Yes, ma'am. We don't often get entertained while we work." The three men marched off like a small platoon of soldiers on a mission.

Caroline sat down at the piano, closed her eyes, and let her fingers move across the keyboard that was home to her. The familiar new melody resonated through the room. No one had heard the wedding song she had composed. This would be the last time she played it until she played it at Rockwater. She played another of her favorite pieces from memory, losing track of time until a knock at the back door returned her to reality. She looked up to see the mantle clock. It had been packed and was gone.

She walked briskly through the kitchen now void of boxes and opened the door. "Hey, Sam. Come in."

"I think I'll do just that. Good heavens, no more maze of boxes."

She followed Sam as he walked through the kitchen and around the counter into the big room. "Yes, they're either stacked on the terrace or in the truck."

The man with the clipboard approached them. "Miss Carlyle, everything's in the van except the piano. We certainly enjoyed your playing, but we really need to finish up and get on our way."

"Sam, let's go sit in the garden and enjoy the sunshine and get out of their way." Caroline grabbed her jacket, unwilling to witness the dismantling of her beloved instrument. It reminded her of the day the piano movers had come to her home in Fernwood to pick up this instrument, her childhood piano. Her parents had sold it to pay for her college education. And then last year, her search for it led her to Roderick. And to Rockwater, where the piano was now returning with her. That made her happy, but thoughts that there'd be no more music in the studio made her sad.

A little while later, the man with the clipboard came to the garden. "Sorry to interrupt, but could we walk through, and then we'll be on our way?"

"Certainly." She rose from the garden bench. "Sam, what time is it?"

"Eleven thirty. Why don't you do your walk-through and join us for lunch? You'll be real lonely in this place without your piano, and you could just plan to stay with us tonight."

"Thanks, Sam. I'll take you up on lunch, but I really want to be here by myself tonight. I have firewood and a couple of books. Besides, I'm getting my hair trimmed late this afternoon, and I have some list-making to do."

Sam chuckled. "You're not going to let Gracie do anything wild are you?

"Not if I can help it."

"And you know she's going to try to wrangle a wedding invitation, don't you?"

Caroline rolled her eyes. "I can handle that. See you in a few minutes for lunch, and I'll bring cookies."

She wished she could handle an anonymous package as easily.

———•———

It was late afternoon. The sun had slipped behind the horizon, and the chill had returned. Caroline drove through

Moss Point slowly, taking the long way around to get to Cuttin' Loose, the salon where Gracie had trimmed her hair for seven years.

The town was beautiful and quaint at Christmas. Oversized fresh green wreaths almost hid the stain-glassed windows of the four churches standing like pillars on the four corners of the town square. The Baptist, Methodist, Lutheran, and Presbyterian church ladies always got together to coordinate their Christmas decorations, and the ministers always gathered to schedule their Christmas programs. For the first Christmas in seven years, Caroline would not be a part of any of those programs.

Caroline giggled aloud to herself when she passed Café on the Square. Mabel had hung her trophy deer head, a twelve-point whitetail, just above the front door. It usually hung on the wall behind the cash register, but when deer season started in the fall, she hung it outside under the awning to remind her patrons she was often hunting early in the mornings and the café might or might not be open. Then at Christmas she taped a red pompom on the deer's nose and hung Christmas bells around its neck. Everyone in town knew that fresh venison was served in the Café during hunting season—deer sausage and fried backstrap smothered in gravy and onions. That's the only way Mabel would cook it. The plates always came with a generous helping of buttered grits and her fluffy biscuits. Nothing green on those plates, but she'd still miss Mabel's comfort food.

Caroline thought of Mabel's Friday-night cheeseburgers and onion rings. *No more of those either where I'm going.*

The small shops lining the streets seemed to make Christmas decorating something between art and a contest, each trying to outdo the other. The Style Shop was the only place in Moss Point to buy fashionable clothes and accessories. Their windows were done in gold and silver trees sitting on a bed of fake snow with headless mannequins dressed in Christmas finery. Selma's decked out their storefront with toys and kid-sized Christmas pajamas and sweaters. And Bishop's Jewelers always had the most elegant garlands framing the rings and watches they hoped would be on the fingers and arms of Moss Point dwellers after the holidays.

Only the spring azaleas and dogwoods lining the streets could rival the spectacle of Moss Point at Christmas. She would miss it, but then she imagined what Christmas would be like at Rockwater. Last Christmas had been nothing short of magical, and she had imagined every detail of her Christmas wedding and what memories it would create.

She pulled into the last empty space in front of Cuttin' Loose. Feeling the eyes of all the town's matrons on her as she walked through the door and to Gracie's chair, she kept her eyes straight ahead. "Good afternoon, Gracie. My hair's a mess, and I've come for my trim."

"Your last trim, I'm supposin', and I agree: your hair's a mess. I think we need to condition it and tame those frizzies. So sorry I won't be there for the weddin', but I could still come if you'd like me to. I could do a fabulous job of your hair and makeup." She shook out a plastic cape and draped it around Caroline.

Gracie had made many suggestions about Caroline's hair through the years. Caroline had succumbed to trimming layers around her face and bangs one time. Disastrous. It took two years for her hair to grow back out. She didn't want to think what she would look like on her wedding day if she turned Gracie loose. "Oh, you're so kind to offer, Gracie. I'm sorry, too, but it's so close to Christmas, and it's nine hours away, and I know how busy you are during the holidays with everyone wanting to look their best for the parties and programs." Caroline didn't want to breathe so that Gracie could start pleading her case again. "But I think you're right about the conditioning. You know what the humidity does to these waves and curls."

"Delia and Gigi and I would have been happy to make the trip, especially if your groom is sending the plane for Sam and Angel. Delia could have covered the wedding for a big spread in the *Moss Point Messenger*, and Gigi would have come along for the ride. She's good with manicures. And I would be there to do your hair and anybody else's." She pulled the scrunchie from Caroline's hair and started brushing.

"Your mama named you right, Gracie. That's so gracious of you, but the wedding will be very simple with just family and close friends. It's going to be in Roderick's home."

She felt the yank of the brush before Gracie lowered the back of the chair, positioned Caroline's head in the bowl, and began the shampooing and conditioning treatment. Caroline relaxed while the water was running and Gracie's mouth wasn't. Then, conditioning done, she followed Gracie to her cubicle for the towel drying, trimming, and styling of her long ringlets.

With no more noise of running water, Gracie continued her probing. "I heard Brother Andy's doing the wedding. So he's going, and I'll bet that house in Kentucky is as big as a church." She picked up her scissors and comb.

"Brother Andy is my pastor, and I've worked with him as the church pianist for years. And Roderick's pastor will share in those responsibilities. And don't lose your money wagering on the size of the house. We'll be setting up chairs in sort of a hallway." It didn't seem right to tell Gracie the hall was a loggia connecting the two large wings of the house. And that it had polished floors made from stone on the property and two-story glass walls overlooking the rolling hills and gardens, and that's where her piano would be home. And no way was she telling her the renovated master suite was twice the size of her studio apartment at Twin Oaks. "Just snip the ends, Gracie. And not too much."

"When are you leaving town?"

"Actually, I leave tomorrow. The movers packed up everything today."

"I know you must be sick of boxes. Saw somebody dropping off a box over there the other night. Or it could have been some guy helping you pack."

"You saw someone with a box?"

"Just for a second. It was dark, and I was driving home."

"Did you recognize this person?"

"No. But then again, as I told you. It was dark, and he had a heavy jacket and hood on. Why do you keep asking?"

Caroline stopped the questioning, not wanting to stimulate more interest in this subject. She wasn't about to tell Gracie of a heart-shaped pillow torn to shreds and a threatening note. "Oh, someone just dropped off a present without a card, and I want to be able to send a proper note." She crossed her fingers under the cape.

"Sure wish you were getting married right here in Moss Point."

"You sound like Angel. And then there's my mother. She's still wondering why I didn't come home to Fernwood. But Roderick and I just wanted something simple and more intimate than a big church wedding. I've been the musician for too many of those."

"Well, honey, it's your wedding. And you should have it just like you want it, even if it does put all your family's Christmas plans in the blender. Just make sure we get to see the pictures." She turned the chair around so that Caroline faced the mirror. "I'll be missing you, you know."

"And I'll miss you, too, Gracie. I don't like the idea of trying to find someone who understands my hair like you do." Seems like she had to keep her fingers crossed most of the time when she was talking to Gracie. Gracie was a good and kind woman. It was just that she only knew how to fix hair that was permed and short and gray.

"You know, you can fly back down here anytime you want to, and I'll have a chair empty and waiting for you." She put her scissors down and removed the cape and shook it. Snips of Caroline's curls scattered across the salon. "I'm assuming you don't want me to blow dry it."

Caroline was anxious to get out of there before any more inquisition. "That's right. I need to get going. It's almost dark, and I'll just let it dry on its own." She reached for her wallet.

Gracie took hold of her hand. "Not today. Just consider this my wedding present. I've always appreciated your business and your music. The town's going to miss you, Caroline."

Caroline stood from the chair and hugged Gracie. She would miss this place, and she would miss Gracie, and she would miss catching up on all the gossip, but she wouldn't miss the interrogation and the nosy inquiries. "Thank you, and Merry Christmas."

Caroline headed straight for the door before anyone else could catch her. She again drove through town on her way home. The streets had been decked out for Christmas since the Friday after Thanksgiving when Moss Point held its annual evening Christmas parade and lit the tree in the town square next to the Civil War statue. No twinkling white lights for Moss Point. Bright red, blue, yellow, green, and purple lights were strung from the tops of the buildings across Main Street. At night it was like driving under a canopy of pure Christmas.

Growing up, she'd thought there was no more beautiful place than Fernwood at Christmas, but moving to Moss Point had given her a new perspective. This street, these lights, the church and store windows, the carillon at the Methodist church, and the music she made here would all be her memories of Christmas in Moss Point. She wondered what her memories of Christmas would be like in ten years.

And she wondered who the person was Gracie had seen dropping off a package at her studio Tuesday evening.

Chapter 5

Leaving Day

———◆———

Friday, December 11
Moss Point

*R*oderick could see the landing strip in the distance and spoke to Acer. "Well, we should get accustomed to this flight and this short runway. If I know Caroline, she'll want to visit Sam and Angel fairly often."

"So I understand. Mr. and Mrs. Meadows are like parents to her, and I can't believe they're entirely happy about her leaving. I'm hoping since he's a judge and seems to run this town, maybe he could get a better runway constructed. Flight's not bad, but landing and takeoff can be a bit challenging"

In another few minutes, the wheels were on the ground, and the engine was idling down. Roderick grabbed his jacket. "Will you secure the plane? I see Caroline's already here to pick us up."

Acer turned off the engine switch. "You got it. And you're sure I'm invited to lunch?"

"As sure as Caroline said it." Roderick released the hatch

and lowered the door for the stairs. Bruce, the one-man airport manager, was already there to lend a hand. Two steps out of the plane and he saw her, standing in the sunshine at the gate to the fence, the window blowing her hair. He still found it difficult to believe how much he loved her. And in one week and one day, she would be his bride. He waved and reached back for his leather jacket.

Caroline met him on the tarmac, and they embraced. "Oh, I'm so glad you're here. I've missed you."

He kissed her and smothered his face in her soft, wavy, sable-colored hair. "No more missing you ever. When we leave Moss Point today, we leave together, never to be parted."

She looked up at him. "Yes, we do. And that's how we'll stay. Together."

"No more long-distance phone calls and no more traveling without you." He took her hand. "Let's get in the car while Acer's taking care of things with Bruce. You'll be warmer there." He opened the car door on the driver's side for her. "I know you want to drive this last drive through Moss Point. Glad you allowed us to come get you. The flight was smooth and beautiful. I'm thinking God is smiling on us. No dark gloomy day for your Rockwater arrival. No long drive, just sunny skies and a short flight."

"The weather would have mattered little as long as we arrive." She took the driver's seat. "Hattie's busy with lunch, and I think it's a big spread from what I've been told. You don't understand that when you request fried chicken it comes with a whole lot of bowls of other goodness. That's Hattie's way." She giggled. "Oh, and Sam told me this morning that Ned and Fred will be there."

"Oh, yes. Ned and Fred, your guardian protectors. They're a couple of real characters."

Caroline cranked the engine and turned on the heater.

"They are that. I think they stood guard for the few hours the movers were here yesterday, not intruding or interfering, just there as though they were making sure everything was done correctly. Sometimes they can be too much help, but those fellows have always been there when I needed them."

"Yes, and I'll always be grateful that they looked after you. Now it's my job."

"The world would be better off if there were more Pendergrass fellows around—just simple, hardworking, honest men. I wonder what'll happen to those twins. They're not getting any younger. They do hard, physical labor, and they can't keep that up much longer." She paused, her gaze thoughtful. "Sam will figure something out. He always does."

———◆———

Fred pulled into the driveway of Twin Oaks in their pea-green pickup. "We're here."

"Looks like it. And I hope you've cooled off a bit. I don't know why you gotta raise such a ruckus about dressin' up. We're sayin' goodbye to Miss Caroline today, and we're askin' her for a big favor, and it don't seem right to do that dressed in overalls. Besides, we ain't workin' today."

"I don't like white shirts."

Ned ran his hand over the crease in his denim jeans. "I don't like starched blue jeans that would stand up in the corner, but we gotta look nice today, like gentlemen. You know Miss Caroline is the only one whoever called us gentlemen, and by crackety, today we're gonna look like gentlemen."

"I'd rather be workin'."

Ned was growing impatient with his twin. "Fred, all you

gotta do is eat and hand her the envelope. You don't have to say nothin'. I'll do the talkin', and the judge will do the rest and clean up what I mess up. I done talked it all over with him. You got the envelope?"

Fred nodded and patted his shirt pocket. He parked the truck and got out.

Ned and Fred walked to the back porch, rang the doorbell, and stood side by side just like they had done for the last four decades waiting on Judge Meadows to either give them their work assignment or give them their day's wages.

Sam answered the door. "Come in, come in, gentlemen. Glad you brought some sunshine our way today."

Fred was silent. Ned spoke. "Yessir. If the pumpkins hadn't already been gathered, there woulda been frost on 'em this mornin'. Are they here yet?"

Sam led them through the kitchen. "On their way from the airport. Caroline just called. Let's go out to the sunroom. Hattie and Angel are like train cars, going and coming from the kitchen to the dining room."

Ned smiled big. "Don't want to be part of no train wreck this mornin'."

"You know this is going to be a real surprise for Caroline. You're still certain this is a firm decision and what you really want to do?"

"Yessir, Judge. Me and Fred done thought about what you said. We talked about it, slept on it, and this is perxactly what we want to do."

"All right, then. After we eat, I'll introduce the subject."

"Aww, Mr. Sam, we 'ppreciate that. You know me and Fred are better at swingin' axes and slingin' weeds than we are at talkin'."

They took their seats in the sunroom to wait for lunch and Caroline's arrival. "Maybe so, Ned. But there's nobody better at thinking than you two. You've thought it through like wise men. Your pa would be mighty proud of what you're doing."

———•———

The only thing left on the chicken platter was the crumbs, and the cornbread was gone. Sam observed the Pendergrass twins and how they enjoyed every bite of Hattie's food. He wondered how long it had been since they had a home-cooked meal outside of what Mabel fed them at Café on the Square. Acer and Roderick weren't shy about eating either. When the meal was done, and before Hattie started serving dessert, Sam spoke.

"Now, I know you can't come back for Christmas—" He nodded at Caroline and Roderick. "—but if you find yourself hungry for black-eyed peas and smoked porkchops, our table will be full on New Year's Day."

Hattie grinned. "You right about that, Mr. Sam. Bad luck to start the New Year without eatin' them black-eyed peas. But Mr. Roderick, since you won't be back for Christmas, I made my famous eight-layer Lane Cake."

Roderick pushed back from the table. "Oh, Hattie. You should have told us about that before I ate that last chicken leg. Lane cake? Don't think I've ever had that before."

"Oh, my Lawd. Then, you'll be wishin' this was your weddin' cake. Some lady over in Columbus named Mrs. Lane won a prize with her recipe a long time ago, but I done made it my own, takin' out the peaches and puttin' in more pecans and bourbon. Next time you head this way, I could use another bottle of Kentucky bourbon."

Sam laughed. "Maybe he should taste the cake first and see if it's worthy of Kentucky bourbon."

Hattie rose from her chair next to Angel. "We ain't

gonna joke about that, Mr. Sam. You know that cake would win a contest if there was one 'cause I got into your Kentucky bourbon."

"Guess I'll be looking for a new hiding place. Just settle down, Hattie. And speaking of settling, maybe we could let that delicious lunch settle some before you cut the cake. And while we're waiting, I'd like to tell you why we've invited Ned and Fred to be our special guests today."

Sam saw the way Angel took Caroline's hand and smiled at her. His anticipation over this surprise had excited him for the last few days. He relished bearing such good news. But the other surprise that had been delivered anonymously to their mailbox earlier this week had not brought with it an eagerness to share. He checked his shirt pocket for the threatening note, the message he had decided to share with only Roderick today.

"Roderick, Caroline's probably told you that Hattie and Ned and Fred are like family to us. These two men were the only ones we trusted to do the work on the park we gave to the town last spring. They cleared the grounds and planted the gardens Angel designed. They have taken care of Twin Oaks like it was their own for about forty years." He looked at the red faces of the twins.

Angel interrupted. "And they built the gazebo in the middle of the park. Did a fabulous job. That's why their names are on the plaque."

Sam nodded. "And they've taken care of our Caroline too. They've been there to help her with her recitals and anything that needed doing around the studio. And she's kept them in homemade cookies."

Ned interrupted. "Yes, sir, Miss Caroline did that, and we gonna miss them cookies."

Sam waited for Ned to continue, but he didn't. "Ned, would you like to say something else to Caroline?"

Ned fumbled with his napkin, wiped his mouth, and took a big swallow of tea. "You know, Miss Caroline, me and Ned are better at other things, not so much at talkin'. But we just want you to know we're gonna miss you, but we're glad the good Lord has made you happy again bringin' Mr. Adair to be your husband."

He looked back at Sam, who nodded encouragingly. "Judge Meadows told us you didn't want no weddin' present. And somehow that just didn't seem right not to give you somethin' to show we're glad you're happy. Ma always gave brides weddin' presents, usually somethin' pretty that she made. We done cut down a tree and sawed it into boards to cure so we can make you a cradle for your first baby. That'll come later when the good Lord decides it's time. But the judge said you had asked for money for the orphan children in Guatemala, so that's what we're givin' you fer now."

Ned looked at Fred. Fred pulled the envelope from his shirt pocket, put it on the table, and pressed the crease out of it with the palm of his hand. He reached across the table and handed it to Caroline.

Caroline smiled. "You are so kind. I just don't know what I would have done without your help since I've been here. You have been wonderful to me and now this. Thank you so much." She folded the envelope and put it next to her plate.

Sam cleared his throat. "Caroline, maybe it would be a good idea for you to open the envelope."

Curious, Caroline did as Sam requested. Her eyes revealed her surprise as she gasped. "Ned, this . . . this is a check for two hundred thousand dollars."

Roderick was silent, but the expression on his face yelled something between shock and surprise. Hattie froze in her tracks and dropped her napkin. "Dear Baby Jesus, that's a lotta grass mowin' and weed eatin'."

Ned was not deterred in continuing his job. "Yes, ma'am. We want to help those children, and we know we can trust you to do that. But we got a big favor to ask you to go along with the money. Mr. Sam, could you talk to her about that?"

"Certainly." Sam leaned forward. "Now, this is a big secret, and you have to promise to keep it or else I'm going to have to shoot you after I tell you, and then you'd miss Hattie's Lane cake."

Angel tapped her plate with her fork. "Out with it, Sam. They're all trustworthy."

"Well, when Ned and Fred were just young boys, their pa bought some stock. Just happened to be Coca-Cola stock."

"Yes, sir. Pa loved them Coca-Colas better than a hog loves slop."

Sam continued. "Yes, he did, and it was a good thing. He kept buying stock all along, and as the company grew in those early days, the stock kept splitting. When Mr. Pendergrass died, he left these men a small fortune. They've told no one except the banker who manages the portfolio and me because we have helped them give the money away in scholarships for years."

Caroline clapped her hands. "You're the benefactors who've been sending Moss Point graduates to college?"

"Why, yes, ma'am. A few of 'em, anyway. The ones we thought might make a difference in the world."

Caroline's smile was big and genuine. "That's just wonderful. And you've managed to keep it secret?"

Sam interrupted, "For the most part. I had to have a little talk with GiGi after she overheard a conversation Ned and I were having at the grand opening of the park last April. What's amazing is that it seems she's kept it quiet."

He saw Ned shaking his head.

"Now, here's the favor. Ned and Fred have set up a family foundation, and they'd like you to sit on the board with them and me. The foundation has about eleven million in assets right now."

Caroline's face stilled as she stared at Ned and Fred. "Me? You want me to sit on the board. But you must know I've never managed more than my own budget."

Fred nodded and Ned spoke. "Yes, ma'am. We trust you and the judge. We watched you and how you treat people. Me and Fred ain't gonna live forever." He shook his head. "Excuse me, we are gonna live forever, but that'll be in heaven. But when we've gone on to Glory, we need somebody young who can keep on givin' Pa's money away."

Caroline swallowed, smiled, and looked at Sam. "If Sam has agreed, then I'd be honored to sit on your board. I'm so grateful for the trust you've placed in me, and I'll do my very best to honor it." She picked up the envelope. "And for this generous gift, I am beyond grateful. You can't imagine what this will do to help."

"It was our first gift out of the foundation. Iffen you don't believe it, look at the check number."

Fred spoke for the first time. "Zero, zero, zero, one."

Caroline opened the envelope again and looked. She rose, went around the table, and leaned over between the twins and hugged them both at the same time. "I'll be forever grateful for the two of you. And now that I'm on the board of the Pendergrass Family Foundation, I'll be seeing you often."

Sam smiled at the thought. "See, Angel, I told you we needed to get some new furniture soon for the studio. Caroline and Roderick will be coming back regularly." He turned to Hattie. "Let's celebrate with some cake and coffee."

Conversation continued around the table. Sam felt a strong sense of satisfaction that all was right in Caroline's world, and he knew that the twins' fortune was now safe and would be used for good for years to come. He and Tom Ellison, the attorney, had made sure of that.

A few minutes later Sam noted that Roderick was looking at his watch. "I'm supposing you folks need to get in the air." But he had another message to deliver.

"Yes, sir, we do." Roderick turned to Angel and Hattie. "This has been such a wonderful meal, and this occasion will be one that Caroline and I will never forget." He turned his attention to Ned and Fred. "Thank you, gentlemen for the ways you've been good to Caroline, and most especially for this generous gift and the confidence you have in her. And Hattie, thank you for frying the chicken. I certainly hope you taught Caroline to do that. And in case you're wondering, your Lane cake is worth a whole case of bourbon. Be on the lookout for its arrival."

They all said their goodbyes, and Sam followed them to Caroline's car and got in. Caroline got into the driver's seat. "Thanks for driving my car back home, Sam. I'm not sure about selling it yet if it's not in your way. It'll be handy when Roderick and I come to visit."

Sam sighed. "Your car will be right here waiting for you just like Angel and I will." He worried there had been no opportunity to talk with Roderick about the letter he'd received. He again fingered the paper in his pocket.

When they reached the airport, Acer and Roderick got out of the car and followed Caroline as she went to open the trunk. She removed a clothes bag. "No peeking. I'll take the dress." She carefully lifted the wedding gown in its bag and headed to the plane. "I'll be back to say goodbye, Sam." She followed Acer, who carried two large boxes.

Roderick continued taking boxes out of the trunk. Sam

walked around to back of the car. "I had intended to speak to you at the house, but there was never a minute. I don't think this is anything worth giving much thought to, but it arrived in our mailbox on Tuesday. No sign of where it came from or who might have sent it. I just thought you should know about it. Maybe you have some ideas about who could've sent it. We don't have time to talk now, but can you call me later when you've had time to think about it?"

Sam saw the puzzled look on Roderick's face. "Caroline knows nothing about this, and as I said, it's probably nothing. But I didn't want to know this and not tell you. Just read it when you get home and give me a call."

"Certainly." Roderick took the folded envelope and stuck it into his jacket pocket.

Sam noted that Caroline was nearing. "You take care of my girl, now, or you and I will be having a conversation and perhaps a sparring match."

Caroline approached as Roderick responded. "Yes, sir. You can rest assured we won't be having that kind of conversation. You can trust me to take care of her, and please know how much I appreciate you and Angel and the way you have loved and cared for Caroline." He shook Sam's hand, and Sam grabbed him for a bear hug.

"And you take care of yourself and sweet Angel. Thanks for everything, Sam. We'll be back for you on Wednesday. Then there's going to be a Rockwater Christmas wedding the likes of which you've never seen." Caroline embraced him, kissed his cheek, and turned to take Roderick's hand.

Sam walked to the driver's side, stuck his cane in the front seat, and got in. He watched as Caroline walked toward the plane hand in hand with Roderick. He stayed until the plane was airborne.

My blue-eyed girl has her wings, and she's flying the nest.

Chapter 6

Home to Rockwater

———— ◆ ————

Friday, December 11
Rockwater

Caroline stepped out of the vehicle and took Roderick's hand. He watched her eyes as she surveyed Rockwater and the surrounding gardens, beautiful even in midwinter. "Welcome to Rockwater, our home, my love."

"This takes my breath away every time. Finally, my dream is becoming my address. And best of all, you're here, and we won't be apart again."

He felt the gentle squeeze of her hand before he dropped it so that his arm could encircle her waist. But when he nudged her forward, her feet remained firmly planted as she gazed toward the front door and surrounding gardens. He could only imagine what she was thinking, but he imagined it was good, perhaps the same kind of disbelief he had in seeing her standing here after all the waiting. "Let's go in. Lilah's been waiting for this since your first arrival to Rockwater a year and a half ago. We shouldn't keep her waiting any longer."

"Shouldn't we save a trip and take a few things with us?"

She turned to walk to the back of the vehicle, but he took her arm and guided her toward the stone path to the front door. "That will all be taken care of. You're home now. Chip will take care of the boxes and bags."

"But my dress." Her look was pleading.

"He takes care of all that you see. I think he can manage your dress." He took her hand again, and she walked beside him.

The entrance was grand with a series of seven semicircular steps, each growing wider as they led to a large terrace. Caroline stopped when they reached the landing to look at the flower beds flanking the stone. "The daylilies and irises are still green."

"Of course they are. They're an evergreen variety. Mother planned the gardens so they'd be beautiful in every season, but it will be springtime before we enjoy the blooms again. Fletcher still works the gardens according to Mother's original plans, but he'll be happy to work with you on your ideas."

Roderick guided her up the narrower next six steps that mimicked the curve of the double front doors. Slender twenty-foot cypress trees framed the entrance. "I don't think I ever told you about the cypress trees. Mother brought them from Europe right after the house was built. She loved the tradition she discovered in the south of France where one cypress planted near the gate or the entrance to a villa was a sign that travelers were welcome to stop for the refreshment of something to drink. Two trees welcomed travelers to drink and eat."

Caroline pointed to the cypress framing one side of the huge window of the dining room. "But I see a third tree."

"Yes, the third tree invited the traveler not only for food and drink but for a place to sleep safely and comfortably for the night. That was my mother. This house always seemed to have interesting people coming and going and a few staying."

"Oh, I wish I had known your mother. I love the stories you tell me about her."

"Yes, and she would love knowing that you will be enjoying the house she designed and built. And she would want you to make it your home. Our home." He punched in numbers on the keypad and opened the door before he turned back to Caroline. "It's also tradition to carry the bride over the threshold, and this seems the most appropriate time to do that since we'll be staying here for the wedding." Before she could respond, his arms encircled her and he was carrying her through the front door. They almost ran into Lilah as he whirled her around before allowing her feet to touch the polished stone floor.

"You're home. Finally. Oh, I'm so happy to see you." Lilah embraced Caroline and held her. Roderick saw the tears dampening Lilah's face.

When Lilah backed away, she kept her hands on Caroline's shoulders. "You just don't know how long I have waited for this day. I have prayed every day since Roderick was born that our good Father would give him a soulmate to bring joy and completion to his life. Finally, my prayers have been answered. You are that answer." She embraced Caroline again.

Caroline whispered. "Thank you, Lilah. Thank you for praying me into Roderick's life. In the so doing, you have prayed him into mine. I will do my best to be worthy of him. Thank you."

Roderick heard her soft words and savored the moment.

Lilah turned to him and wiped her eyes with her handkerchief. "I guess you just jumped the gun and brought your bride over the threshold according to tradition."

"I confess."

"Well, does that mean you kidnapped your bride like they did centuries ago? Or were you just avoiding bad luck by not taking the chance she'd trip and fall coming through the door?"

"Neither. I just wanted to hold her in my arms." He put his arm around Caroline again.

Lilah stuffed her folded handkerchief under the cuff of her sweater. "Good boy. No such thing as bad luck, not when the Lord's in charge. And from the looks of the smile on her face, you didn't have to kidnap her."

They laughed together, and Roderick coveted the joy of this moment and the hope of the future.

"Could you call Chip to get her bags out of the truck?"

"Already done. He's on his way up from the barn."

"Thanks." Roderick looked around the loggia. "I see the movers have been here."

"Been here and unloaded. Everything they brought is stacked in the dining room, Caroline. We'll get to the unpacking tomorrow, but for right now, I just want to enjoy knowing you're here. Chip will bring in your personal items, and we'll put them in the upstairs guest suite, the one where you always stay, unless you've changed your mind and want to put your things in the master suite." Lilah looked at Roderick.

"No, ma'am. I'll take the guest suite for now. But I can hardly wait to see what they've done to the master suite. Roderick's had no time to give me the details."

Roderick looked down the hall. "Did they finish?"

"Finishing touches just before lunch. The furniture has been rearranged a bit. The painting, bedding, and draperies are gorgeous, and the bathroom update looks like a magazine spread. Then there's the surprise Roderick planned for you. I think you'll find everything just like you imagined, Caroline."

"Surprise? I have a surprise for Caroline?" Roderick saw the delight on her face. "Just so you know, I haven't seen the room since they finished the demolition and construction and the painting. I was waiting for you so we could see it finished together."

"Wait! Demolition and construction? I thought they were painting, putting in new flooring, new draperies, and a few cosmetic things. Now you tell me construction?"

"You can't remake a bathroom without construction. Shall we see it now?"

"Oh, yes."

Roderick took her hand and led her down the hallway to the suite with Lilah trailing behind. He opened the double wooden doors and welcomed her.

Caroline hesitated slightly before walking in and quickly glanced around the room. "Ooh! You're right, Lilah, it's beautiful. Those blush-colored walls, and the coral silk draperies and sheers . . . And the bedding! It's so lush and gorgeous." She turned to the fireplace. "Oh, and look at the fabric on the chair and the chaise. The colors are so warm and light. And that paisley turned out even better than I thought." She turned to Roderick. "I remembered you really like paisley."

Then she looked above the fireplace, her breath caught between inhaling the surprise and exhaling more disbelief.

Her silence brought Roderick to her side. "If you re-member, Sarah only wanted us not to dispose of Mother's portrait and the rope swing out back. The portrait of my mother is now in the library, and I replaced it with this portrait of you. And Angel's portrait of you will hang beside my mother's. So now Sarah can enjoy them both."

Caroline didn't move, other than her eyes, which traced every curve and line of the painting.

"I took photos of you at the piano in that stunning pink gown when you were here for your first recital. I sent those photos to the same artist my father commissioned to paint my mother's portrait. Actually, Lilah remembered him, and we were able to find him in upstate New York. I want to see you in that pink gown at the piano when I turn out the light at night, and I want to see it in the first rays of morning light. This portrait is my gift to myself."

"Roderick. Would I sound too proud to say that it's beautiful?" She fumbled for words. "I mean the painting is beautiful."

"Then you like it?"

"I love it."

"That makes me so happy. Now, let's see the surprise for you."

They walked into the renovated bathroom they had designed together. Caroline had remained insistent that the bathroom entrance to the walled garden and outdoor shower stay the same. "Everything was done exactly as we planned except for this." He led her to the wall behind her dressing table. "This bathroom was so spacious that it allowed for redesigning this closet space."

He opened the door to a spacious room lined with shelves, shoe racks, built-in furniture, space to hang clothing, and a sizable, marble-topped island in the middle. "This, my dear, is our walk-in closet." He delighted in watching Caroline peruse the space. "I think you'll find there's a place for everything, from your shoes to your jackets to your jewelry." He stepped to the island and started to open a drawer."

Lilah quickly stepped in front of him. "This is a grand closet. Tomorrow, I'll help you unpack your boxes and move your things in here. We'll leave a bit of space for Roderick." She swept her hand across the marble on top of the island. "Roderick designed this so that you can put your suitcase right here to make packing easy for all these trips you'll be taking."

Roderick recognized Lilah's look and followed her lead. "Just a bit of space?"

Caroline grinned. "I would never have dreamed of anything so grand, and there's plenty of space for both of us."

"I'm glad for that, and I enjoyed making this happen. And I think my mother would be more than pleased with everything we have done." He looked at his watch. "And speaking of making things happen. I need to make a quick phone call. Maybe you two could brew us a cup of coffee or tea and hopefully find a cookie. I'll be back as soon as I can."

———•———

Roderick slipped quickly down the hallway, through the kitchen, and out the door and across the courtyard separating the house from his apartment. He needed privacy for this call.

He sat at this desk, pulled the folded letter Sam had given him from his pocket, and dialed Leo, head of security for Adair Enterprises. He read the letter again, stopping at the last sentence, and rereading it until Leo answered.

"We have a problem, and I need you to check it out." He read the letter to Leo. "It was delivered to the Meadows' mailbox without postage or return address. I think I know who might have done this. Can you come by in the morning and pick it up? I want it checked for prints or for anything else you might find." He paused. "Do you have any ideas or are you thinking the same thing as I am? Liz Bevins. She never liked it that I didn't become personally or romantically involved with her. I think she's had it out for Caroline since day one, and then when I fired her for not following my instructions in planning Caroline's trip to Guatemala, that made matters worse. She raised a ruckus, telling me what a mistake I was making and that Caroline was not the woman I should be marrying. I helped her get a job in Richmond, mostly to get her away from here. But this just has the look and sound of her."

"Could be, but why don't I come by later this evening to pick it up and check it out?"

He folded the letter and put it back into the envelope. "That's not necessary, and I have plans. Tomorrow's good enough. I think Liz is harmless, but she went to a lot of trouble to deliver this letter. The wedding is only a week away, and I want to ward off any trouble."

"There'll be no trouble, Boss." Leo's voice was confident. "See you around eight in the morning."

——·——

Lilah offered to prepare a light dinner, but Caroline noticed Roderick's wink at Lilah when he insisted that he would take care of it. While he busied himself in the kitchen, Caroline unpacked the things she needed for the night. She practically ran down when she heard him at the bottom of the stairs, inviting her to dinner. "Meet me in the morning room for an early-evening dinner if you dare."

They dined at the table in the morning room next to the kitchen. An early dinner in front of the picture window afforded them the opportunity to watch the sun set behind the hills in the distance—the same hills that would be covered in Kentucky bluegrass and yellow daffodils in April, according to Roderick.

Caroline took the last bite of her sandwich. "Tomato soup and a grilled three-cheese sandwich? Some couples have songs. I guess we have a special dinner."

"It seems to be our favorite. I remember every detail of the evening we returned to Atlanta after I flew you to Fernwood when little David was born. The hotel restaurant was closed, but I persuaded the chef to prepare a grilled cheese for us, and afterward, we sat out on the terrace under the full moon and had a cup of tea while the sycamore leaves rained on us."

"That was a night to remember." Caroline gazed at him fondly.

"I'll say. Although I think I knew it when you played your recital in the pink dress, that night in Atlanta was the first time I could say to myself that I truly loved you, and the moon hasn't looked the same since."

"And I realized that same night that I loved you."

"I wish you had told me. It would have saved me nights of pacing and handwringing. I loved you so much that it frightened me, and I didn't want to alarm you by moving too fast."

Caroline grinned sheepishly. "Too fast? The looks on my face practically begged you to kiss me that night, but you didn't."

"Oh, it was not from lack of wanting to. That was the most restraint I've ever practiced. What frightened me more was doing anything to dissuade you from continuing our relationship."

Caroline gazed into the distance at the last rays of sun. "Seems we both knew it and were afraid." She leaned closer to Roderick sitting beside her and put her head on his shoulder. "But here we are at Rockwater together, eating another grilled-cheese sandwich you prepared for us, and we're one week away from getting married."

He caressed her cheek. "An unbelievable dream come true. Last summer when I thought I'd lost you in Guatemala, I couldn't bear to think that you'd never be at Rockwater with me again. I've never prayed so fervently. But I don't want to think of that, for we have so many utterly beautiful moments to remember."

She raised her head and took his hand. "Oh, yes, that surprising proposal dinner where you arranged for Hattie and Ned and Fred to provide our dinner. A bowl of soup and a grilled-cheese sandwich just like tonight." She pointed to the silver dome in the center of the table. "The Baby Ruth? That's what we had for dessert when you proposed."

Roderick reached for the handle on the dome and lifted it, revealing a dozen Baby Ruths stacked on a platter.

"Wow. This stash should last me at least until the wedding." She looked longingly into his eyes. Her heart was so full—full of love, full of newness, full of gratitude, and full of disbelief that this could be her life. Her eyes welled with tears as she reached for the candy. "Roderick, you are so good to me. This evening is absolutely perfect."

"It's perfect because you're finally here with me. Help me get the dishes cleaned up. I'll make us a cup of hot chocolate to go with our fancy dessert, and we can sit by the fire in the library and talk about tomorrow and all the beautiful evenings we will have right here in this place.

Chapter 7

Unpacking Boxes and Secrets

———————◆———————

Saturday, December 12
Rockwater

*E*ven after a perfect evening with Caroline in the library, with Christmas music playing and seasoned oak crackling and turning to embers as they talked about the wedding and future nights, Roderick spent a restless night, staring across the courtyard at the soft light in the window of the guest room where she slept. All night, he tussled with the blanket and grappled with what to do about the letter.

He rose early. After shaving, he stared in the mirror at the bags under his eyes. *Is this the face of the man who keeps secrets to protect his bride, or is it the face of one who tells the truth to earn her trust?* He dressed quickly, putting the letter in the pocket of his jeans. He grabbed his sweater and walked across the courtyard to the main house.

The lights were on in the kitchen. He could see Caroline putting a tray of something in the oven. He didn't recall that Lilah had left anything for their Saturday-morning breakfast and had planned to cook it himself. He knocked on the door so that his surprise entrance before daylight wouldn't startle her. "Good morning, my love. Cooking breakfast already?"

She turned and greeted him with a good-morning kiss. "I'm practicing. Only one week left to get this cooking-for-my-husband thing perfected."

He rounded the island to the stove. "What's in the oven?"

"Biscuits." She rinsed her hands after cracking the eggs.

"Real, made-from-scratch biscuits?" He turned and leaned against the counter.

"Yep, just the way Mother Martha makes them. And cheese grits and scrambled eggs and bacon."

"You mean your mom's biscuits?"

Caroline nodded. "The very same. At home, her biscuits are legendary, and she's known as Mother Martha."

"Now I'm really impressed." He picked up the kitchen towel and brushed the flour from her cheek.

"Thanks, just don't expect this every morning. There are such things as yogurt and granola and fresh fruit, you know. Then I wouldn't have flour on my face and buttermilk on my apron." She took the towel from him and popped his leg with it.

He loved everything about her. Her gentleness. Her playfulness. Her seriousness. Her passion about music and all things beautiful and those she loved.

Last evening, they'd watched the sun set behind the hills as they ate their dinner in the morning room. This morning, she had set the table next to the window in the gathering room so they could enjoy the sunrise. They ate and talked lightheartedly until finally he pushed away from the table and wiped the last biscuit crumbs and jelly from his mouth. "Again. I'm impressed. You said you could cook, but you really can cook. Can't wait to see how you and Lilah will work out this whole who's-going-to-cook thing." He grinned.

He noticed she didn't smile and that a seriousness had replaced her playfulness.

"So, today we're going to unpack your things and put everything away?" he asked.

"That's the plan. I tried to tell Lilah that you and I could handle it, but she insisted on returning. However, she did agree to let me cook breakfast. I told her I'd save her a plate."

"Already working it out, I see."

"Um-huh." She stared out the window and became quiet.

He watched her face in the morning light, wondering what had captured her thoughts. "Looks like you just went somewhere. Take me with you."

She wasn't smiling when she faced him. "You are always with me wherever I am." She paused. "There is something I need to tell you. I didn't want to tell you on the phone, and I didn't want anything to disturb our first evening alone at Rockwater, which was a most beautiful evening, by the way."

"It was, and the first of thousands to come. But now you have me worried. You're not backing out on me, are you?"

He saw the muscles in her face relax. "Not in a million years."

"Good. Nothing else really matters, so now you can tell me what you didn't want to tell me."

He leaned forward and propped his elbows on the table as she began to describe the box that had been anonymously delivered to her studio. By the time she finished describing the heart-shaped pillow that had been ripped apart, his insides were writhing. "Tell me again exactly what the note said."

"If I'm remembering correctly, it said, 'If you marry Roderick Adair, this will be your future.'"

"And no return address or delivery label?"

She nodded in agreement. "Only Betsy knows about the box. She was the one who found it at the terrace door when she arrived on Tuesday night. I didn't want to tell you, but Betsy insisted." She looked away. "It wasn't that I would keep a secret from you, but I just didn't want it to mar our wedding. And I didn't tell Sam and Angel either. They don't need to be worried about some threat that's just a sick joke."

Roderick pulled the letter from the back pocket of his jeans. "Seems we were both trying to protect each other and our beautiful wedding plans."

He saw the questioning in her eyes. "What is that?"

"It's a letter Sam received on the same day you received your package. He didn't want to bother you with it, but apparently the same person who left your package left this anonymous letter in his mailbox. He gave it to me yesterday because he wanted me to know." He handed her the letter.

She read it slowly and put it on the table. "Do you have any idea who might have done this?"

"As a matter of fact, I do. I think it might have been Liz Bevins. I called Leo yesterday afternoon, and he'll be here around eight this morning to pick the letter up. I want this checked out."

"But why would she go to all this trouble?"

"I think she might have had thoughts that something personal could develop between us—her and me, I mean. I never, ever gave her any reason to think that, but I'm sure you must have sensed Liz was very jealous of you. She was angry when I fired her after that near tragedy in Guatemala when she didn't follow my instructions. I did help her get a job in Richmond just to get her away from here." He picked up the letter, put it into the envelope, and laid it on the table.

"You think she'd go to all this trouble to scare me away?"

"I'm not sure what to think, but Leo's going to check it all out. He'll find out if she was in Moss Point on Tuesday. And there could be some fingerprints on the letter. If it's Liz, then she did break a law by putting that letter in Sam's mailbox." He paused. "What did you do with the box?"

"I sealed it up and put in the trash with the rest of the stuff left over from the packing."

"Would it still be there?"

"Possibly. They don't pick up trash until Tuesday, but there was so much trash that Sam could have had Ned and Fred haul it off."

"Mind if I call him and ask?" Roderick looked at his watch. "Leo will be here in half an hour, and I'd like to talk to Sam before he gets here."

"Sure. Since Sam already knows about the letter, there's no need to hide this if it might help find who did it. I'll clear the table and get us another cup of coffee while you call him."

Caroline picked up the plates and mugs and headed to the kitchen. Roderick pulled out his cellphone and called Sam. She returned a few minutes later with two steaming mugs of coffee.

Roderick was still on the phone. "Hold on, Sam. She's back." He said to her, "Boxes are still there and Sam wants to know if you remember the size or anything else about the box."

"It wasn't large, maybe ten-by-fourteen inches and four to six inches deep. I know that it was a plain box, no marking of any kind."

Roderick repeated her answer to Sam. "Okay, Sam. We'll get to the bottom of this. Sorry you had to be bothered with this nonsense." He put his phone away.

Caroline sat down across the table from him. "So he's going to look for the box."

"He's planning to call Ned and Fred to find it and haul the rest of the trash off." He looked at her. "I don't think that I thanked you properly for breakfast. It was the best. Thank you, and thank you for not hiding this from me." He paused and sat back in his chair. "Now, I need to know something. Does this box or letter cause you to have any question about us?"

She didn't hesitate. "Absolutely not. The only question I had was when to tell you about the box. I know, Roderick, in a marriage that honors God, there must be no secrets. I have no secrets from you. I have shared my past and my feelings and everything there is to know about me with you. I trust you completely."

He rose, walked around the table, and knelt in front of her. He took both her hands, kissed them, and held them. "Caroline, how I love you. But I confess that being completely honest with you is a real struggle for me, not because I would ever want to hide anything from you but because I want to protect you. I want you to be happy and safe and never worried or fearful. That's my role as your husband: to make you smile and to take away anything that would make you sad or worried."

She blinked the tears her eyes. "I love you for that, Roderick, but that's not your role as my husband. Your role is to love and trust me with whatever comes. That's the for-better-or-worse part. We can't protect each other from life's ills and pains, but as husband and wife we have each other during those times. I know you're a powerful man who makes things happen, but not even God protects us from troubles. But He is ever present when they come. I'm grateful you want to make me smile, but I'm more grateful you want to be by my side."

"Always and forever." They stood facing each other in front of the window. He pushed her wavy, sable-colored curls from her face and kissed her before burying his face in her tresses.

———•———

Leo arrived. Caroline had not seen him since the day he flew home with them from Guatemala. She served him coffee. "It won't be as good as the coffee in Guatemala, but we're in a much safer place to drink it. At least I think it's safer."

Leo chuckled. "Oh, it's safer all right." They remained in the kitchen while she and Roderick gave him the story about the box and the letter. Leo put his mug on the kitchen counter. "Don't want either of you worrying about this. It's a piece of cake after your kidnapping in Guatemala, and I'll get to the bottom of it right away. Don't know what' I'll be able to get done before Monday, though."

They were finishing up when Lilah arrived. Leo took the letter and was out the door. Lilah stood at the end of the kitchen counter with one hand on her hip and pointing her finger at Roderick. "I got the tail end of that conversation, but you know as well as I do who did this—that red-clawed, green-faced Liz Bevins. No need to look further than her. She was trouble in high heels when she walked in the door, and I'm hand-raising happy she's out of here."

Caroline watched as Lilah began wiping the counters with the dishrag. "Lilah, we've had breakfast, and I've already cleaned the counters."

"Sorry. Wiping is just what I do when I'd like to mop this floor and the whole county with that woman. I clean something else whether it needs it or not." Lilah stopped. "I'm done with this now. That woman is not going to steal our joy. Not the joy of your beautiful wedding day nor the joy of moving your things into the master suite today. I'm ready to go to work."

"But I saved you a plate for your breakfast." Caroline retrieved the plate from the oven and led Lilah to the barstool. "Sit down and eat. We have work to do. And tell me how you like your coffee?" She put the plate in front of Lilah.

Roderick perched himself next to Lilah on the barstool. "Just cream, please."

Caroline caught how Lilah looked at Roderick and smiled when she said, "Somehow, this doesn't seem right, but I think I'm going to like it."

———◆———

Lilah soon finished her breakfast. "My goodness, you can cook a biscuit, girl. Now you go do what you need to do. I'll clean up after myself, and we'll meet in the dining room and get this unpacking done this morning. And Roderick, do I need to call Chip?"

"No, ma'am. I'm here to do the hauling and unpacking if you ladies can manage getting things organized in the closet and whatever else we need to do."

Caroline responded shyly. "It's mostly clothes and books. I did bring a few of my favorite things from my kitchen, though, if there's room."

Lilah responded. "Sweetie, there's room for anything and everything you bring into this house. It's your house. Now go brush your teeth, and let's get busy."

Caroline left the kitchen, calling over her shoulder to Roderick. "Ten minutes. In the dining room with gloves on."

"Yes, Miss Blue Eyes. Lilah told me I wasn't going to be the only boss around here."

Once Caroline had gone, Roderick quickly came to Lilah's side at the sink and spoke softly. "About yesterday, when we were in the closet and I was about to open the drawer, I followed your lead, but what was that all about? We had it all planned."

Lilah whispered back, "We did, but now we have a change of plans. I got to thinking about it, and our plans just didn't seem right." She dried her hands and put the towel away.

"You want to tell me what the new plan is?"

"I do not, but I'll show you." She led him into the office off the kitchen. "Hurry! Before Caroline gets back."

Chapter 8

One Never Forgets Happy Times

———— ◆ ————

Sunday, December 13
Rockwater

The fog and flurries crept in like shadows over the horizon Sunday morning. Roderick stopped the truck in the lane and pointed in the distance. "Look, there's a bit of snow accumulating on the roof of the covered bridge."

"Let me get a picture." Caroline leaned as far as she could out the truck window to take the photo. "Do you think we'll have a white Christmas for our wedding?"

"Possible. This morning's flurries won't last long because the temperature's warming, but there's another front on the way. Acer's keeping a careful watch since we'll be flying on Wednesday to pick up your parents and Sam and Angel."

Brushing the snowflakes from her coat sleeve, she closed the window. "I'm praying for a perfect snow, but maybe I should pray for sunshine with all the folks traveling."

He pulled slowly down the lane and through the covered bridge. "Sarah and George's afternoon flight should be fine. And they'll take good care of Bella and Gretchen. I'm glad they'll be with us for three nights before moving to the Castle for the rest of the week."

"I don't understand why they don't stay at Rockwater. There's plenty of room."

"Not unless you move into the master suite. Besides, Sarah is insisting on being the host for the rest of the family and friends who are staying at the Castle. She wants to make certain everything is perfect for all our guests, and we'll make certain your parents and Sam and Angel are comfortable with us at the house."

"God bless Sarah. I don't know what I would have done without her during the wedding planning and renovations at the house. She's the sister I always wanted."

"And Sarah feels the same about you."

The view of the church in the distance reminded Caroline of a Christmas card. It was small, quaint, surrounded by a white picket fence, and housed a bell in the steeple that could be heard on the nearby farms. It was ringing through the Kentucky hills this gray December morning as local congregants gathered.

Reverend Thomas greeted them as they entered. "I'm so happy to see you two. This is a big week, and Caroline, you'll be happy to know I've spoken with Brother Andy several times now. I can tell you your wedding will make beautiful memories."

"I'm so happy to hear that. It's important to the both of us to have our ministers doing this together."

Since the death of his father, Roderick had not been a frequent church attender. With several nods and smiles to people he obviously knew, he led her through the sanctuary without stopping. There would come the time for him to introduce Caroline to them, but they were running a bit late. They took their seats in a pew, not a seat in church that Caroline was accustomed to. As church pianist for years, Sundays in December had been busy days with extra music for worship and Christmas concerts.

This morning, she sat proudly next to Roderick, enjoying the candles and wreaths in the stained-glass windows and the organ almost humming "O Come, O Come, Emanuel." She held his hand and thought of Sundays to come when they would worship together and baptize their children, and perhaps she might be invited to sing or play on occasion. Her life was changing in so many ways, and all those ways seemed good.

With the last amen and bells ringing in the steeple, they dashed to the truck through the grayish brown slush that had been white only an hour ago. Roderick cranked the truck and sat quietly for a moment. "You know, I had all but stopped going to church. Too many memories of my parents, two funerals, and I could remember my mother singing, and I would feel so alone sitting on that pew by myself. But today was a different experience. Thank you for bringing church back into my life."

She pondered his words. She had gone to church alone for the last seven years yet never felt alone. "You're welcome. Church is where we'll both have friends, and we'll make some happy new memories."

"To celebrate going to church together here for the first time, I'm taking you to the Castle over in Versailles for brunch. It's only about a ten-minute drive. They have the best Belgian waffles. And while we're there, I can take care of last-minute arrangements for our wedding guests so Sarah won't have to do that." He took her hand and kissed it.

"Betsy says that's all that Josefina has been talking about for weeks. Nothing about Santa or Christmas, just about being the flower girl and staying in a castle like a princess."

"Then, let's make sure everything is magical for all of them." Roderick dialed the number for the Castle to reserve a table and pulled out of the church parking lot.

———·———

"What time is it," asked Caroline as she and Roderick returned to Rockwater.

He looked at his watch. "Almost two o'clock. What do you say let's change out of these fancy duds into something comfortable, and I'll build a fire for us in the library? Sarah and the others won't be here until around five. So we can nap by the fire."

"That sounds like a December-Sunday-afternoon thing to do. While you build the fire, I'll get the soup on."

"Soup? You're making soup. I was planning to take everyone out tonight." He recognized the raising of her right eyebrow.

"Well, I was planning to make soup and a big pan of cornbread. It's cold, and they'll be tired. This way, we can stay in and all enjoy the fire."

He put his arms around her, pulled her close, and kissed her. "Then we'll have soup. And maybe you and Bella could play the two pianos for us."

"That can be arranged."

"Do I need to go to the store to get what you need to make the soup?"

"Ah, no. You see there's this curse I have. It's called planning. I called ahead, and Lilah was kind enough to add the things I requested to her grocery shopping list on Thursday."

"You two *are* figuring it out." He smiled and released her. "I'll put on some jeans and be back shortly. If you're lucky, you might get me to chop the onions." He winked at her and was out the door.

He changed into jeans and a sweater hurriedly, went to his desk, and dialed Sam's number. An idea had come to him in the middle of the night.

Sam answered. "Hello and Merry Christmas, whoever you are."

"And Merry Christmas to you, Sam. It's Roderick. Hope your Sunday is as fine as ours. Just wanted to report that Leo is working on the letter and box issue. He'll get to the bottom of this, but he couldn't really get too much done on the weekend. And the second thing is I need a favor."

"You got it, son."

"I'd like to surprise Caroline, and really I'd like to surprise Ned and Fred by flying them up for the wedding. They have entrusted so much to Caroline, and they have protected and helped her these last several years. The wedding is small, with just family and a very few friends, but those men seem to be like family to you and Angel and Caroline."

"That's a mighty generous thing for you to do. You know, I doubt those fellows have ever been out of the county. No, I forgot. A cousin took them to Atlanta for a Braves game. But I'm not sure if Fred can contain himself flying on a private plane. He gets all lathered up about engines and vehicles."

Roderick adjusted his collar underneath his sweater. "Do you think they'd come?"

"Of course they'll come. I'll put the two of them on the plane myself if I must. I'm glad you called me today, though. I may need to take them to town to get suits and a few other things tomorrow. I don't think I've ever seen them in anything but overalls and blue jeans. They even wear them to church with a starched white shirt."

Roderick chuckled. "Overalls will be fine. Just get them

red bow ties. There's no one coming to the wedding who would be surprised. And please tell them I've made all the arrangements and they're invited out to Rockwater on Friday night for our Christmas gathering. They don't need to bring presents. All they need to do is get on the plane, and I'll take care of the rest."

"Man, am I going to love this. Ned and Fred flying to Kentucky and putting on a suit. Can't wait 'til ol' GiGi finds out about this."

Roderick imagined Sam's belly was shaking, he was laughing so hard. "GiGi?"

"You remember GiGi, the orange-haired town gossip and man-chasing floozy." He cleared his throat. "Well, it was orange the last time I saw her. Lord, forgive me for saying such unkind things, but I speak the truth. And to make matters worse, she's the one who found out the Pendergrass twins are rich when she overheard Ned and me talking at the park opening. Right then and there, she set her hat for Fred, chasing him like a hound dog after a jack rabbit. Why, that woman was like a cat waiting for milk to be poured into her bowl, but Ned's lawyer and I took care of that. When I made sure that GiGi knew she'd never see a penny of that money and threatened her if she divulged the secret, she quit chasing after Fred. But she'll turn red and green when she hears those boys are going to the wedding and she and Gracie didn't get an invite. Whoopee! You made my day, son."

Roderick didn't miss that Sam called him son twice. Hearing that made *his* day. It had been a long time since anyone called him anything that familial. "I'm glad I could make your day by asking you for a favor. I'd best get back over to the kitchen. I promised Caroline I'd chop onions for the soup. If I hear anything from Leo tomorrow, I'll give you a call. Otherwise, I'll see you on Wednesday. I'll call with the details."

——·——

Ham and lentil soup simmered. Christmas music resonated softly through the halls and the library. The lights on all the Christmas trees twinkled, and the scent of pine and cedar wafted through the whole house. Almost every room had its own Christmas tree and garlands on the windows. Caroline knew she had made the right decision. No need for extra wedding decorations. The house was beautifully dressed for Christmas.

Roderick and Caroline cuddled under her favorite afghan on the sofa. Comfortable in his arms, she was in that nether world between sweet sleep and satisfying thoughts of her new reality. She had planned one spring wedding that never happened because David was killed. And now her Christmas and wedding plans were made, and she was here with Roderick. Almost all items on her to-do list had checks beside them, and she intended to enjoy this week.

Everything she owned was now at Rockwater, and her heart had truly moved in as well. *By this time next Sunday, I will be Mrs. Roderick Adair, and all our family will be gone, and it will be just the two of us figuring out how to maneuver daily life. And we'll have our very first Christmas right here, no one else, just us.* Like vapor, her thoughts drifted until she fell asleep.

She was awakened by a slamming door and rose from the sofa quickly. "Rod, we're here!" She recognized Sarah's voice.

"Finally, you're here. We've been waiting all afternoon." She winked at Roderick, walking beside her on their way to the foyer.

Bella rushed around Gretchen to get to Caroline. "My goodness, I think you've grown another inch since I saw you last," Caroline laughed. She kissed Bella's cheek before Bella reached for Roderick.

Caroline greeted Gretchen and Sarah and George before getting them to their rooms. She said to Sarah, "I can't wait to show you what we've done with the master suite, but let's get you settled first."

The guests went to their suites to unpack, and Caroline and Roderick went to the kitchen to finish up the soup and cornbread. It was only minutes before she heard Bella playing the piano. Still, she could hardly believe how gifted Bella was and how much progress she was making at Duke. Hearing Bella play one song, "David's Song," had changed all their lives a year and a half ago. That moment in time had solved questions for her. It had freed Gretchen and Bella. And it had engaged Roderick and Sarah in all their lives in ways she never could have imagined. She knew that only God could have orchestrated something so unusual.

After dinner, they settled in the library for the evening, Roderick and Caroline on the sofa, Sarah and George on the loveseat, and Gretchen in the wing chair next to the fireplace. Bella moved back and forth from the sofa to the loggia to play the piano. Everyone's faces mirrored their happy, contented hearts as they spoke of the wedding and of Christmas.

As the evening waned, Sarah pulled a small box from behind a cushion on the loveseat. "I have something for you, Caroline. Remember, you asked me a few weeks ago if Mother used handkerchiefs and if I still had one." She walked over and handed the box to Caroline. "Not only did I find one of Mother's linen handkerchiefs, I found one belonging to our maternal grandmother, and I brought one of mine. Amazing what people store in cedar chests. I found some other heirlooms I'll share with you another time. So now with your mother's and both your grandmothers' handkerchiefs, you're going to have a whole bridal bouquet of linen and lace and white irises."

Caroline opened the box. "Oh, they're beautiful." She gently ran her fingers along the soft fabrics. "I'm so happy you found them, and thank you for bringing one of yours. I'll return them to you after the wedding."

Sarah smiled warmly. "No need to do that. They're still in the family when they're with you."

Caroline held the handkerchiefs near her face and smelled the cedar. "Thank you, Sarah. I'll definitely figure out something special to do with them."

Gretchen reached into the pocket of her sweater and pulled out a small parcel wrapped in white tissue paper. "And my friend, would you give me the pleasure of adding another one to your bouquet? Sarah told me what you were planning." She rose from her chair to hand the small package to Caroline.

Caroline unwrapped it carefully and unfolded the handkerchief. "This is exquisite, Gretchen. It will mean so much to me to know I'm holding all of these in my hands on my wedding day. Thank you so much." She fought back happy tears.

Gretchen leaned to kiss Caroline's forehead. "And it will mean much to me, my friend. When Sarah told me your plans, I asked her to take me to a shop where I found some fine Irish linen. I made you this handkerchief and tatted the lace edging. It's the pattern that my grandmamá taught me when I was a child."

"And you remembered how to make it?"

"Oh, yes. Those were such happy days spent with Grandmammá. One never forgets such times. I can hardly wait for our trip to Austria in the spring when I will show you where I spent so many blissful times."

Caroline leaned back into the sofa and Roderick's arm. She pondered. *One never forgets such happy times.* *A wedding at Christmas. What could be a happier time?*

Chapter 9

Surprises

———◆———

Monday, December 14
Moss Point

*M*onday morning brought blue skies and a brisk, stiff wind to Moss Point. Fred stoked the fire, turned on the television for the news, and sat down in his wooden rocker with his coffee mug.

Ned rushed into the room. "Turn off that TV and put yer shoes on. We goin' to town."

"I know we goin' to town to put up the Christmas lights at Twin Oaks, but I ain't goin' nowhere 'til I finish my second cup."

"You don't know nothin'. I mean we goin' to *town* town. Mr. Sam done called this mornin', and you ain't gonna believe this, brother. That Mr. Roderick called Mr. Sam yestiddy and invited us to the weddin'. He says we are like family and he wants us to come and surprise Miss Caroline."

Fred stopped rocking and didn't move a muscle.

"That's why we goin' to town. Judge Meadows is takin'

us to get some clothes to wear. We goin' on a trip, Fred, a real trip."

Fred still didn't move a muscle. He didn't even blink.

"Did you hear what I said?" Ned walked across the room and stood between his twin and the television. "I said, put yer shoes on. We gotta make some tracks."

Fred grumbled. "I ain't goin'."

"You can take your dadburned coffee to town with you. Let's go."

"I said I ain't goin'."

"You sick or somethin'?"

"No. I'll go to town, but I ain't goin' to Kentucky. I ain't never been to but one weddin', and I ain't goin' to no second one. Besides, I don't know iffen our truck would even make it to Kentucky."

"Well, you can mark that one off yer worry list. We'll be flyin' on Mr. Roderick's plane with the judge and Miss Angel." He knew that would get his brother. "And that's that. We ain't about to disappoint Mr. Roderick and Miss Caroline. So git up. We gittin' new clothes and Christmas presents for ever'body. I done counted 'em up. We need six presents. Then, when we git through with all that, we'll put up the tree and the Christmas lights for Miss Angel. And it's my year to untangle the lights and yer year to plug 'em in to see if they work."

Fred sat up straight in his chair. "We flyin' on that plane? For real?"

"Yep. Jus' like real gentlemen, all dressed up and on a plane."

Fred started putting on his shoes and mumbled with excitement. "We flyin' on a plane. Ain't that finer than frog hair?" He got up. "I'll be back in a minute. I need somethin' off the back porch."

With his brother out of the room, Ned closed the screen

doors in front of the fireplace and turned off the television. Fred returned in less than a minute with a coffee can in his hand. "How many people you say we gotta get presents fer?" He removed the plastic lid.

"Six. Why?"

"I'll go to the weddin'. And I'll go to town to git some clothes. And I'll hang Miss Angel's Christmas lights, but I ain't shoppin' for no Christmas presents." He opened the can and started counting out hundred dollar bills. "We'll give 'em money. Ever'body likes money, and we don't know nothin' about shoppin' for no women." Fred kept counting. He handed a stack of bills to Ned. "Here's six thousand dollars. That's a thousand apiece, then they can go git whatever they want."

"Where'd you git all that money?"

"Outta the freezer."

"I mean, where did this money come from?"

"I been savin' it from all them tin cans I been recyclin'."

"That's a lotta tin cans, Fred."

"Yep, and there's more where this came from." Fred put the plastic top back on the can.

The two put on their identical plaid wool jackets, and Fred drove them to town. Ned did all the talking on the drive in, describing the clothes Judge Meadows said they'd need and when they'd be leaving and returning from Kentucky. "By the way, brother, where'd you say you keep that coffee can?"

"In the freezer on the back porch."

"That's crazy, Fred. They ain't even a lock on that screen door."

"I know."

"But somebody could walk right in there and steal yer money while we're gone."

"Nobody ever did in fifteen years. Besides, I figgered

iffen somebody took somethin' from the freezer, they was hungry. And iffen they took the money, they might need that too."

———•———

Ferngrove

Martha stood at the base of the attic ladder. "Thomas, I know the box up is there. Look over near the dormer window. It has her name on it in big bold letters."

Moments later Thomas came down the ladder balancing a box on top of his head with one hand. "Got it. What a brother won't do for his sister who's tying the knot." He put the box down on the floor in the hallway and brushed the dust from his hands. "I'm just glad she's finally getting married. Otherwise, this box and all its contents would be disintegrated from the heat in that attic in a few more years."

"Maybe the carton, but not the contents. Every ornament is individually wrapped and sealed in individual boxes—all twenty-nine of them."

"I remember you gave Callie and me my box of ornaments when we got married. If you hadn't, our tree would have been decorated with tin foil and candy canes. Where do you want the box?"

"Take it to the mudroom. I don't want dust everywhere." Martha followed her son. "Just put it on the floor. I need to get the ornaments out."

Thomas opened the carton for her. She carefully took them out one by one and stacked the small boxes on the cabinet. "Now take this nasty carton to the shop please. Your dad's out there. And could you bring me the chest he built for the ornaments?"

"What? Dad built a chest for Caroline? My ornaments came in a cardboard box. She's getting how many? Twenty-nine? And I didn't get but twenty-two?"

Martha swished him with the kitchen towel. He dodged her. "Well, you shouldn't have gotten married so young. Your dad wasn't retired when you and Callie married. Now he's got time, and he wanted to build this Christmas chest for your sister. Besides, every ornament I made for you and James was made with just as much love. Now, go get the box he made. I have a ton of things to do."

Thomas returned moments later. "I thought you said this thing was a chest. Never saw a chest with a hinged, cushioned lid covered in fabric before. It's a stool. She can sit on the thing."

"It's your sister's. She can do whatever she wants to with it. But she'll know your dad and I made the box and everything in it just for her. It's made of wood from a walnut tree on your grandfather's place. That makes it even more special." She started hauling the smaller boxes into the kitchen. "Bring it in here. I need to get all these wrapped and put in the box and check this off my list. And one more thing, then you can go. I know you must have things to do today."

"Just a few." He set the walnut chest on the breakfast table. "What's the one more thing?"

"I have two fruit cakes in the cabinet above the oven. If you could get one of them down for me, then I won't have to climb the stool and hope I make it down with the cake in one piece."

Thomas opened the cabinet and got the foil-covered fruitcake. "But it's not Christmas. What do want with the fruitcake? We never cut it before Christmas Eve."

"When they were here for Thanksgiving, Roderick requested a fruitcake for their Christmas. So, Caroline and I made the fruitcakes like we always do on the day after Thanksgiving."

"Oh, that's right. He asked you to bring one last year to surprise Caroline because she had told him it was our tradition."

"Yes, he did."

Thomas took a big whiff of the fruitcake before putting it on the counter. "Smelling good, but not like homemade plum wine."

"Probably because it's wrapped in cheesecloth soaked in Angel's peach brandy. I use the plum wine when I don't have peach brandy." Martha began wiping the dust from every ornament box with her dishtowel.

"This cake will have that plane of his smelling like a Carlyle Christmas."

"Don't worry. We'll have our cake for Christmas like we always do. We just won't have Caroline here with us. Maybe next year."

Thomas hugged his mama. "So, you're driving to Moss Point tomorrow? What time are you leaving?"

"Planning to leave right after lunch. We'll enjoy the evening with Sam and Angel, and then Roderick will pick us up early Wednesday morning."

"Well, I guess the next time I see you will be in Kentucky. And don't you fret, Mother Martha. We're going to have a fine time celebrating Christmas at Rockwater, and then we'll have our family Christmas at home." Thomas sauntered out the back door.

Martha sat at her kitchen table and opened the remaining boxes, remembering Christmases past, and recalling how she'd spent weeks gluing sequins, sewing pearls, crocheting bells, and making a new ornament for each of her children every Christmas until they married. James and Thomas had their ornaments, and now, it was time to give Caroline hers and hope she would carry on the tradition with her own children.

I should have known this time last year when she went to Rockwater to play her recital and stayed for Christmas that Christmas for the Carlyle family was about to change. An even bigger change for my precious daughter.

———•———

Rockwater

Roderick's first order of business early Monday morning was to call Leo. He wasn't certain what he expected, nor did he think that Leo could have found anything out over the weekend. But he called anyway. He tapped his deck with his pen, counting taps until Leo answered.

"Good morning, Leo. I know it was the weekend and you probably don't know anything yet, but I wanted to know what you're planning."

Roderick continued his pen tapping while Leo reported. "You're right, sir. I don't have any information yet, but I did make a couple of calls on Saturday to get the plates spinning first thing this morning. I have a man checking on Ms. Bevins' whereabouts on the date in question. He's using cell phone and credit card records. And a discreet phone call might just be made to her new job for information if need be."

"Seems simple enough. And if it's not Liz?"

"Well, sir, I have the letter, checking it for prints. Should know something about that maybe tomorrow or Wednesday. Somehow, I don't see Liz Bevins doing this. She's a smart woman—not without guile, but smart. I've been thinking all weekend about this, and it just doesn't make sense. She'd be risking a lot with nothing to gain. Oh, and it would help to have the box."

"Sam's on top of that. He'll find it." Roderick stood and circled his desk.

"Look, Roderick. We've brought that young woman from the bowels of Guatemala, and we're not about to let anything happen to spoil your wedding day. Just in case we can't get this figured out before then, what I am planning is extra security for the estate. I'm lining it up, but it's going to cost a bit extra since it's the holidays."

Roderick sat at his desk again. "Whatever it takes. Let's get this solved. I know I can count on you, Leo. Keep me informed. Goodbye."

————•————

Monday afternoon at Rockwater was quiet. The last meeting with the caterer was done. Roderick and Sarah were in Lexington checking on arrangements for the Wednesday-evening party they were hosting for their friends and Roderick's business associates. George was out in Roderick's apartment studying. Lilah was directing the last decorating touches. Bella's piano playing filled the halls with music. That left Caroline free to visit with Gretchen in the morning room.

"So much has happened since we were here last Christmas." Gretchen sipped her tea.

"Who could have imagined? I still can't believe that my search for my childhood piano brought me here. I have wondered what would have happened if I had given up finding it."

"Yes, your search brought you back to your piano and to your heart, my friend. It was God's plan to bring joy into your life. And if you had given up, then God would have found another way to bring you happiness."

"I'm glad I didn't give up and stuck to His original plan." Caroline couldn't keep from smiling. "And I'll be so happy knowing that Bella is playing my grand piano. Everything is set with the movers." Caroline munched on a cookie.

"Yes, we will be there when they bring it in next week."

"Oh, I wish I could be there to see Bella when it's delivered! Maybe Karina could take some pictures."

"Certainly. Karina is adjusting so well, excelling in all her classes at Duke, and then she is so helpful to me in the bakery in between her classes and studying. She has immersed herself in learning all she can about savant syndrome, and she comes home and tells me everything she has learned. She is so good and patient with Bella."

"That's wonderful, Gretchen. Your deep joy is written all over your face." She took the last sip of her tea and rose from the morning-room table. "The piano was the first secret. Now I have another. Follow me."

She walked through the kitchen and down the hallway to the loggia and to her pianos. She sat down at the piano Bella wasn't playing and waited for her to finish Debussy's "Arabesque Number One." "Do you mind if I join you? You've been serenading us, so now it's my turn. Gretchen, take the chair over there." She pointed to the chair she'd brought from her studio that now had a new home next to her piano here in front of the window.

Bella silently and mechanically removed her hands from the keyboard and placed them in her lap. Their eyes met and they looked intently at each other as Caroline began to play. Then Caroline closed her eyes as her hands caressed the chords from her piano and her voice soared like the clearest church bell in the large hall, the phrases rising and falling until the last note. There was a moment of stillness when she finished. She opened her eyes, looked at Bella still sitting like a statue at the piano facing her. She turned to see Gretchen's face.

Gretchen dabbed her eyes. "Your wedding gift to Roderick?"

Caroline's voice, as smooth as silk while singing, now cracked. "Yes."

"It is more than beautiful, Caroline. It comes from the depths of your being and speaks of the purest love. It will be such a gift for him and for all of us to hear it on your wedding day." She leaned forward in her seat. "Does he know?"

"No. I want to surprise him."

Gretchen rose from the chair and joined Caroline at the piano. She touched Caroline's cheek gently, tucking away a tendril of curly hair behind Caroline's ear. "I do not bring this to your thoughts to make you sad. But you wrote "David's Song" as your wedding gift to David. When he died, you did not finish it. For seven more years, you did not finish it. It was in this room that you finished it when you came here the first time. Your heart had to let David go to make room for another. And now you'll be singing your wedding song to Roderick."

Caroline stood from the piano and embraced Gretchen. Her face trembled as her tears began to flow. Not sad tears, but tears from an overflowing heart. "I was so sad for so long. My grief consumed me, all of me, and I cried rivers. The real music in my life was gone, and I just went through the motions and accepted I would never be happy again." She became quiet, her chin resting on Gretchen's shoulder.

Gretchen did not break the silence.

Caroline released her. "Now, my heart is so full and I am so happy, and I'm still crying."

Gretchen pulled a tissue from her sweater pocket and

handed it to Caroline. "Yes, dear one, but your tears come from a very different place in your heart. I know because my own tears of sadness have turned to tears of joy."

Caroline was wiping her eyes when she heard familiar sounds coming from the piano. She turned to see Bella playing just before Bella began to sing. Caroline whispered to Gretchen. "Oh, perhaps I have made a big mistake in playing this for you. I forgot. Bella has heard my song, and now she will play and sing it perfectly." She and Gretchen held hands and laughed and listened to Bella until she finished and turned to them with her twelve-year-old grin on her face.

Caroline sat back down on the piano bench, and they began to play together. For a few moments, time was suspended and the present was magical. When they resolved the last phrase, they smiled at each other, knowing the sheer joy of the moment.

Caroline turned to Gretchen "Now we have a problem. How do we keep this human tape recorder from spoiling my wedding surprise for Roderick?"

Chapter 10

Rings and Things

———◆———

Tuesday morning, December 15
Rockwater

*R*oderick breathed a sigh of ease when he received a call from Mr. Harrigan early Tuesday morning. Although he had a couple of options from his mother's jewelry, he wanted Caroline to have her engagement ring for the party on Wednesday. Roderick parked his truck right outside Harrigan's Jewelers. A bell rang as he opened the glass door to the shop.

Mrs. Harrigan, an elegantly dressed white-haired woman, greeted him. "Good morning, Roderick. I am so happy to see you this cold December morning. You're like warm sunshine. Let me get Marshall for you. He's in the back huddled over his drawing table designing something, but I know he'll want to hand your package to you himself."

"Thank you. I'm anxious to see it." He perused the collection of estate jewelry in the glass cases as he waited.

Mr. Harrigan, stooped and hobbling in with a cane, looked over his wire-rim glasses as he entered the room.

"Roderick, my boy. I'm relieved to be able to deliver this package to you." He walked to a table and sat down on a stool. When Roderick took the antique chair opposite him, Mr. Harrigan opened a small velvet-covered box and pulled out the engagement ring, which was now finished, and the wedding ring. "It took a while to find these rare pink diamonds, especially the baguettes to channel set for the wedding ring. But they arrived from Australia, and I have set them in rose gold just like the engagement ring. I must say they are exquisite. You are a man with fine tastes, just like your father, Roderick."

"Thank you, but like my father, I'm marrying a rare woman who deserves something that is matchless." Roderick extended his hand across the counter.

"Well, these are matchless and rare, and sized correctly to be worn on a small, delicate finger." He placed the rings in Roderick's left palm.

"She's diminutive but big hearted." Roderick picked up the engagement ring to examine it. "You were right about the rare pink pearl needing to be surrounded by pink diamonds. Perfect. And the cut of the baguettes spaced with the smaller round diamonds for the band . . . What can I say? More perfection." He handed the rings back to the jeweler. "She will love them. And one of the reasons I love her so is that she would appreciate a plain gold band."

"A rare woman, indeed. Let me get this boxed for you. And I'll get the papers for their authenticity." He returned the rings to the velvet box. "Your other package is all wrapped, and Mrs. Harrigan was able to find an antique box like Lilah requested. The other items have been polished and placed in it, and they're ready to go. The necklace is wrapped separately inside."

"I'm grateful for the meticulous care you take, Mr. Harrigan. Lilah and I will be very happy. I'll be in touch."

Roderick settled the transaction and drove home listening to the recording of Caroline's "Rockwater Suite" she had composed for him and debuted at her recital last February. His heart hummed the melody with joy. Four more days until this wedding band would encircle her finger.

Driving into Rockwater knowing that Caroline was there made his heart content. He parked his truck and quickly secured the wedding band and the wooden chest in the safe in his apartment and walked over to main house. He could hear the piano when he entered the kitchen door and found Caroline with Sarah and Gretchen in the morning room.

Caroline sprang from her seat, went to Roderick, and kissed him lightly.

He knew he would never tire of the way she greeted him. "If that's the kind of greeting I get, I think I'll go out and come back in again. Ladies, I need to steal Caroline away for just a few minutes." He took her hand.

She followed without hesitation. "Where have you been this morning? I've missed you."

"It's Christmas. You shouldn't be asking questions like that, but you'll find out soon enough." He led her through the loggia into the library. As they walked by the piano, he said, "Bella, that's beautiful music you're playing this morning."

Bella continued playing as though someone had switched on her Play button, paying him no mind.

They entered the library. "Here, sit with me. I had to make a trip to town this morning. I was getting so worried about your ring, but here it is." He pulled the box out of his vest pocket and opened it. "Just in time, the diamonds have all been replaced with the pink ones from Australia."

"Oh, let me see." She took the ring from the box and took a deep breath. "It is truly beautiful, so different with these stones and the warmth of the rose gold."

"Mr. Harrigan knows his jewelry, and I know you. I know you didn't expect a ring like this, which makes it so much more meaningful for me to give it to you. I feel like I need to get down on one knee again."

"No need for that. Just put it on my finger and tell me you'll never take it off again."

He slid the ring on her finger, squeezed her hand, and kissed her longingly. He held her face in his hands, savoring the moment. "And Bella is playing such beautiful music as a backdrop for this scene this morning." He saw the look of alarm on Caroline's face when Bella started to sing.

Caroline bolted out the door to the piano. "Oh, no."

———•———

Moss Point

Sam looked at his watch when the phone rang. Ten o'clock sharp. He liked that Roderick was a man of his word. "Good morning, Roderick."

"Good morning to you, Sam. I'm calling in as I said I would. Not that I have much to report."

"I sat on the judge's bench for decades, and as many lies and half truths as I've heard, I appreciate a man who'll do what he says and tells you the truth even if it's not what you want to hear. So, do you know anything?"

"Leo was on top of this all day yesterday. The one we suspected, my former assistant, was not in or near Moss Point on the day the letter and the package was delivered. She was in Richmond where she works. He checked her phone records, her credit-card activity, and finally called her office discreetly. She did not make the delivery."

"Mmm-huh. Now, if it wasn't this woman, do you have

any other ideas?"

"I didn't say it wasn't this woman. Liz is capable of hiring this done in a way that her hands remain clean. Leo's still working on it, but it's not as simple as we hoped."

"Nothing ever is. You don't think she'd make a scene at the wedding, do you?"

"Not a chance. Rockwater is secure every day, but Leo is using extra security on the wedding day to ensure it's perfect, just the kind of day Caroline and I want."

"Then I'll quit worrying and mumbling to myself about this. I know you have it handled. See you tomorrow."

Angel walked in as he was hanging up. "I'm ready. Can you drop me off at the beauty shop?"

"Yes, ma'am. But you're mighty beautiful just as you are." He winked at her. "Just talked to Roderick. Nothing yet on the letter and package. Doesn't look like the person he suspected is the guilty one." He followed Angel, her red purse swinging on her arm, out the kitchen door to the car.

———•———

Sam drove right to the front door of the shop and stopped. Angel leaned over for him to kiss her cheek. "I'll call you when I'm done. Just make sure Ned and Fred will be finished with the decorations by lunch. I want everything done before we leave for Rockwater, and I'd like this afternoon to rest and be ready for J. and Martha's arrival. And remind Ned to be on time in the morning and to search the trash for the infamous box."

Sam grinned. "Do you really think those men will be late tomorrow? Ned already told me this morning their bags are packed. Why, they probably won't even sleep. Check that off your worry list. They won't be late."

Angel got out of the car and walked into Cuttin' Loose with a secret smile on her face. She had a plan. Maybe Roderick couldn't find out who the culprit was, but if it was someone in Moss Point, she knew how to find out.

"Good morning, Mrs. Meadows." Gracie hugged Angel.

"Good morning to you, Gracie." She followed Gracie to her station and plopped herself down in the zebra-striped chair. "Let's get this done and over with. I have other things to do today."

Gracie draped a leopard-print plastic cape around Angel. "Would you like me to do some color with this trip and fancy wedding and all?"

"Gracie, dear one, you ask me that every week even if I'm going to the grocery store, and the answer is always the same. No. Anything you do to this white hair turns it bluish purple, and I'm not going to Rockwater looking like a turnip root. Just wash it, roll it up, set it, and get me out of here."

Although she pouted, Gracie took her at her word and was soon smoothing Angel's white hair over pink plastic curlers. "I sure wish Caroline was getting married here so we could all attend."

Angel smiled her secret smile again, knowing that was one reason Caroline was getting married in Rockwater. "Well, that sweet girl wanted something simple and small. I guess with her years as a musician, she's seen far too many wedding fiascos."

"I didn't think about that."

Angel took a deep breath before she set her plan in motion. "Now, Gracie, you can't tell a soul, but I'm just praying that this one won't be a fiasco either." She told Gracie about the letter put in their mailbox and the package and note Caroline had received. "Why, we just couldn't believe it! Roderick seems to think that it could be someone who worked for him that he fired. I just don't know, and I'm worried nearly to death about it. It was very frightening with that threat and all." Angel knew she was putting it on thick.

"Well, I never. That's just the meanest thing I heard since old man Terrell tried to run his wife crazy with that tape recorder of his." Gracie kept rolling hair.

"That was mean, and this is against the law to put a letter in somebody's mailbox. If it's the woman he fired, Roderick will see to it that woman is put in jail for upsetting Caroline. Now you don't tell a soul about this. There's no need in anybody knowing. I just wish Caroline didn't have to give this a thought. Poor girl. She's had enough tragedy in her life."

Gracie finished rolling Angel's hair and sat her under the dryer. Angel grinned on the inside, knowing that her secret would seep through the cubicles at Cuttin' Loose and would be oozing down the streets of Moss Point before dark. If the culprit was someone local, Gracie would know it first. Angel knew from Sam that Gracie had alerted the police to lots of mischief by keeping her ears open in the beauty shop.

Hair dried. Rollers out. Hair brushed, back combed and sprayed stiffer than Ned's and Fred's starched white shirts. Gracie handed Angel the mirror and twirled her around. "Your hair will look like this for the wedding Saturday if you just sleep in that satin bonnet."

"That I'll do." Angel stood up, reached in her bag for cash, and pulled out a red envelope with extra cash in a Christmas card. "Hope you have a Merry Christmas." She leaned close to Gracie and whispered, "And remember, not a word about the letter and package we received."

——·——

Rockwater

Sarah was grateful for a few moments alone with Caroline. She ran her hand along the arm of the chaise lounge. "Caroline, Mother would love what you've done with the master suite, especially since you kept the colors warm and light. Your portrait is exquisite, and I'm so happy with Mother's portrait in the library with Dad's. That's where it always belonged, but Rod couldn't bear to move it." She paused. "You used the muted paisley." She looked at Caroline. "Just another way to let me know how much you love my brother. He still wears Dad's paisley ties, you know."

"I do know. What a relief that you like what we've done."

Sarah wanted Caroline to feel comfortable and make this her home. "Oh, I do." Sarah sat down in the chair next to the fireplace. "Sit with me for just a few minutes."

Caroline sat on the end of the chaise. "Will I need a tissue for this?"

Sarah had never spoken of these things with Caroline, but it was time. "Perhaps. You must know that Roderick and I have so many memories attached to Rockwater— memories of festive Christmases and Mother's musical soirees, as she called them. She lit up not just a room but the whole house with her vivaciousness. And then there were just the quiet family times in the library, which always seemed to be the place we were together, reading or playing board games. But when Mother died, Roderick felt responsible because he had insisted they go riding that afternoon. And when the storm came up and the horse threw her, my dear little brother held her for two hours in the rain until someone found them. He didn't speak for a year, and my dad was never quite the same. Dad tried, but his heart was so wounded. In a way, we lost both our parents that day. Sorrow replaced all the joy we once had here." Sarah wiped a tear from her cheek.

"I cannot begin to imagine the sadness. Children should not have to bear such tragedy."

Sarah looked into Caroline's eyes. "I didn't really mean to become so morbid. I say all this to tell you how grateful I am you and Roderick found each other. You bring the joy and music back into these Rockwater halls that have been hollow for so long, and you have brought real life to Roderick." She stood, walked to the window, and looked out across the hills. "I've tried to be a good big sister, but I must tell you I've had to speak rather harshly to him about giving himself to Adair Enterprises. It was his escape from real living, just one business conquest after another, but now he looks forward to the future. A future with you." She turned back to look at Caroline. "Thank you for loving him so much. He treasures you and trusts you with his heart. I know that you will be gentle with him."

Caroline stood and joined Sarah at the window. "I love him more than I could have ever imagined. I know the pain of loss, and on Saturday, I will promise to Roderick in the presence of all who love him that I will cherish him and every moment we have together." She hugged Sarah.

Trying to lighten the moment, Sarah giggled. "And I'm getting you as my sister. I love Roderick, but I always wanted a sister."

Caroline added, "Me too. We have fabulous brothers, and now each of us has a fabulous sister."

Sarah turned to face Caroline and smiled broadly. "And on another happy note, just to give you a report. With your help and Reyna's guidance with the paperwork, George and

I are making progress on adopting Rosita. We're hoping to finalize everything in February. Sister Gabriela has been such a help in keeping us in contact with Rosita and preparing her for her new life. I do hope you and Roderick will go down with us to bring her home."

Caroline closed her eyes and sighed. "Of course, we'll go. I really could use that time to attend to some business there as well. But, oh, what a blessed child Rosita will be with you as her mother!"

Sarah took Caroline's hand and started walking toward the door. "We have begun Skyping with her, and it's amazing how much English she's learning. Sister Gabriela is really helping with that. It will make the transition so much easier if she knows some English."

"You're so right. When my friends Betsy and Mason adopted their daughter, Josefina, she had not yet begun to talk. That made things much easier. But it will be a bit different with Rosita. I hope that Rosita and Josefina will become friends."

"We'll make certain of it. And I'll be meeting Josefina in just a couple of days." She paused and looked at Caroline again. "We have prayed for a child for so long. And to think of the strong connection with you since your shared experience in Guatemala, and you'll be her aunt, and she'll be part of our family forever. I can hardly wait to introduce her to Bella and to Josefina. It just all seems so right."

"Because it is right for so many reasons. I couldn't be happier for you, Sarah."

Sarah led her to the door. "We must get on the road. I'd like to get to the Lexington Manor before dark. That way Gretchen and Bella will get to see the grounds and get settled before we go to dinner. Then we'll all be moving to the Castle on Thursday."

"I'm sorry you're leaving to make room for my parents

and Sam and Angel, but I must tell you I'm grateful you're taking Bella and Gretchen or else I'd have to lock both pianos to keep Bella from giving my surprise away."

"Surprise?"

"Don't ask. Our wedding and Christmas are on the way. Not a time to be inquiring about surprises."

Chapter 11

Expectations and
Unexpected Arrivals

————◆————

Wednesday, December 16
Rockwater

Caroline and Roderick sat at the island in the kitchen. Lilah poured them each a cup of coffee and handed Roderick a brown bag. "Here you go—a warm muffin with eggs and bacon for breakfast on the run. Now you're certain I don't need to prepare lunch?"

Caroline responded. "Oh, for goodness sake, no, ma'am. You're entirely too busy this morning. My head is hanging with guilt that I won't be here to help you. I know the decorating is finished, but all those linens from the guest rooms need changing." Caroline peeked into the bag and looked at Lilah. "Ah . . . I only see one muffin in here."

Lilah saw the puzzled look on her face and looked sheepishly at Roderick. "Well, no need for you to feel guilty, and there's only one muffin because I thought you'd be here with me this morning."

Caroline looked at Roderick. "I assumed I was going. I'm not going?"

He took her hand. "Oh, my sweet. I assumed you'd have things to do to get ready for the arrival of your parents and Sam and Angel, and then there's the party this evening."

"I know, but I thought I'd be going with you. There's room on the plane, isn't there?"

"Barely. They are bringing their luggage and Christmas with them remember. It will be such a quick trip, and we'll be back by early afternoon. We'll stop and have lunch in Lexington. You and Lilah can have the house all to yourselves this morning."

Lilah knew about Roderick's surprise and thought he needed rescuing. "If you really want to go, maybe I can call my niece or a cousin to come out and help me. Lots of beds to change this morning." She watched Caroline's face expression turn from disappointment to acceptance.

"No, I'll stay with you if Roderick will hurry home." Caroline tapped Roderick's nose with her index finger. "Get going, you soon-to-be-husband of mine. Lilah and I will spend the morning rearranging all the furniture."

He stood, pinched her chin, and kissed her goodbye. "Wherever you want the furniture is where it will be. Just don't hurt yourself. I'll call you along the way. Love you both." He was out the door.

Lilah brought two plates and sat down next to Caroline. "Would you have breakfast with me before we start to work?"

"My pleasure. And you're using the Christmas china this morning."

They scarfed down the muffins and scrambled eggs and bacon amid conversation about the morning's activities and last-minute preparations.

"I'll be running in to town later this afternoon," Lilah

noted at one point. "If you'll get me all the handkerchiefs going in your bridal bouquet, I'll take them by the florist."

"About the handkerchiefs . . . I was wondering if you have one that I could use. You've been such a constant and abiding person in Roderick's life and now mine. It would mean so much."

"Why, dear one, that's about the sweetest thing I've ever heard. I'll be certain to add one of mine when I take them to the florist. It'll make me so happy to see mine there next to the handkerchiefs of the women that you and Roderick love so much. Lilah rose, leaned to kiss Caroline's cheek, and picked up their empty plates, heading to the sink.

Caroline followed. "No, no. Let me do the cleaning up. You did the cooking."

Lilah smiled. "Four hands make a quicker finish." They worked together like well-oiled gears. "I do have ears, and I think I know something that I'm not supposed to know, so forgive me. I think I've heard you singing a beautiful song that sounded like a wedding song." She saw Caroline blush. "And I think I heard Bella singing it too."

"Yes, you're right. And I'm relieved Sarah took Gretchen and Bella with her yesterday before Bella spoiled my wedding gift surprise for Roderick. I've written our Christmas love song. You must have heard me when I played it for Gretchen."

"I did, but not all of it. Would you play it for me now? You might not have any more time before the wedding to practice." Lilah put the dishtowel on the counter. "Come, my little songbird. This will be my break before starting to work this morning."

Caroline did as Lilah requested, glad for the opportunity to sit at her piano. "I don't need to practice. I went to a recording studio in Atlanta and recorded this with piano and a few strings. Brother Andy will have it cued up to play at the right time, but I'll play and sing it for you." She closed her eyes as her fingers found their home on the keyboard.

Lilah contemplated as she listened. She remembered an afternoon of singing simple hymns and gospel songs right here in this room with Caroline playing. And this same gifted musician had composed a complex and exquisite work using images and sounds to commemorate her love for Roderick. When Caroline finished, almost breathless with tears rolling down her brown cheeks, Lilah stepped behind her and wrapped her arms around Caroline's shoulders. "That, my girl, is beyond beautiful, tying love being born at Christmas with your love for Roderick. I'll have boxes of tissues for all our guests because there won't be one dry eye in this room. And you may need some of those handkerchiefs in your bridal bouquet to dry Roderick's tears. That music will move him deeply, Caroline. I don't know how you do it."

Caroline turned around and took Lilah's hands. "This song came so differently than most. Sometimes a song starts with just a snip of a melody or a couple of melodic phrases. Sometimes it might start with the lyrics. But this all came together in a rush, and I've made very few changes to it in its creation."

"Inspired. Truly inspired." Lilah hesitated. "Would you consider saving the recording for Roderick? I'll wrap it up beautifully for you to give to him. Then you could play and sing it for your wedding just as you played it for me now."

"Oh . . . I've thought about that, but I'd really like to see Roderick's face when he hears it. And honestly, I'm not sure I could get through it without tears myself. I find it nigh on to impossible to sing with a big lump in my throat."

Lilah cautiously added, "I was thinking . . . it was the good Lord using this piano to bring you two together. It was right here in this spot that Roderick fell in love with you in that pink gown. It was the same night you said your goodbyes to David when you finished his song and opened your heart to Roderick. This is hallowed ground, Caroline."

"It is, isn't it. There is something almost sacred about this place, and truly God has done some work here. I'll think about it, but please don't be disappointed if I use the recording."

Lilah clapped her hands together and smiled broadly. "You'll do what's right. Now, why don't you just sit here and play and enjoy yourself. I'll gather the laundry from upstairs and get the washing started. Then I need to go out to the barn and check on the tack room."

"I've been in the barn, but I don't think I've seen the tack room. By the way, what is a tack room?"

"It's basically a storage room for saddles and medicines and the stuff you need with horses, but Roderick made himself a small apartment there years ago. He lived in it until his cottage was built out back. I just need to get to the barn and check with Chip about a few things, then I'll be back. You make music while the sheets are washing, you hear? We'll finish upstairs when I get back."

Lilah knew there'd be guests in Roderick's apartment tonight and he'd be sleeping in the tack room again, but she wasn't about to spoil Roderick's surprise. She took advantage of the moment to stop by the cottage to pick up one more gift he had for Caroline.

Lilah mumbled to herself as she walked out the door. "Surprises, surprises. Heads are going to spinning with surprises."

Caroline played the piano until Lilah returned. Then they headed upstairs to finish tidying the guest rooms. With the last sheets on the guest bed, Caroline looked at the clock on the mantle in the green suite. "Where did the morning go? It's nearly one o'clock. Roderick said they'd be here by two. I think I'll take a warm soak and be ready when my parents arrive, and I won't be so rushed to get ready for the party."

"You do just that, and I'll run my errand and try to get back before our guests arrive. I saw the handkerchiefs you left in the kitchen. I'll get them to the florist, along with mine." Lilah grabbed her dust rag and cleaning caddy and headed downstairs.

Caroline heard Lilah leave and watched her drive down the lane from the bay window in the bathroom. As bubbles filled the marble bathtub, she stood at the window gazing out on acres of Rockwater and imagining what it would be like in the spring.

When the tub was close to overflowing, she stepped in and let the warm water and bubbles cover her. She closed her eyes and relaxed. This was the very first time she had been alone in her new home. It felt good but strange. *What will I do with myself every day as the mistress of this manor? I have no students or rehearsals. I'll have no need to practice. I have no friends here. Maybe I can begin composing again.*

She sank deeper into the tub and imagined a day from sunrise to sunset and wondered how long it would be before it truly felt like home. Even with its opulence, Rockwater was a warm, inviting dwelling. She wanted it always to be the place that she and Roderick most felt at home with each other.

Fifteen minutes passed before she opened her eyes and rose from the water. She quickly dried her hair and was putting on jeans and a sweater when she heard the door followed by Roderick's velvety baritone voice. "Caroline, I'm home."

"Caroline, I'm home." She smiled and whispered to herself. "Roderick, I'm home too." In her excitement, she almost skipped down the stairs to the foyer.

In seconds, Roderick's arms encircled Caroline, and he kissed her cheek. "I was about to think you had gone with Lilah to town. Look who's here." He released her and moved to the side.

"I was here all by myself, but not anymore." Caroline hugged her mom and dad and Sam and Angel. "Oh, I'm so glad you're finally here. I hope the trip was without mishap."

Caroline's mother patted Roderick's shoulder. "It was perfect. No turbulence, and what fun."

"It was a perfect day for flying. And by the way, we even picked up a couple of hitchhikers." Roderick opened the door. "Come on in. Welcome to Rockwater, gentlemen."

Caroline was obviously shocked and totally delighted as Ned and Fred stepped into the foyer like wooden soldiers. They stood side by side with matching green sweaters and khaki pants. No John Deere caps. Hair slicked down with something greasy. She had never seen them in anything but overalls. "Hitchhikers, you say. Well, they're the finest-looking hitchhikers I've ever seen, and I couldn't be happier that you're here." She rushed to embrace them and then turned to Roderick. "What a wonderful surprise!"

He took her hand. "Ned and Fred have been your guardians for years, and they've made you a guardian of sorts. They're like family, and our wedding is a family affair. I wanted to surprise you, and they accepted my invitation."

Ned spoke. "We're mighty grateful to be included in such a momentous occasion. Why Fred and I have been accused of gamophobia, and I guess we are. But we ain't when it comes to you and Mr. Adair here. Besides, we wanted to come and check this place out and make for certain you was goin' to be all right."

Caroline saw Angel reach for the pad and pencil in her purse. She knew Angel had been keeping up with Ned's new-word obsession for months now. "You have no worry. As you can see, I'm going to be more than all right here."

Roderick led the way. "Let's get you all settled in your rooms, and then maybe we can come down to the morning room for a cup of tea or hot chocolate." He pointed out the large loggia window. "Ned and Fred, just across the courtyard is my cottage where I've been living for the past several years. You'll be staying there. But I thought you might want to walk through and see where the Carlyles and the Meadowses will be staying."

Ned answered, "Yes, sir. We'd like that. We're just a couple of old apple-knockers, and we ain't ever seen no place like this one. But maybe we should go and get the suitcases first."

"No need for that, Chip will have all your luggage in your rooms in just a bit. He's coming up from the barn."

Roderick led them through the loggia, pointing out the library and the master suite and the guest room downstairs where Angel and Sam would be. Caroline followed them and heard Fred whispering to his brother. She would have given two bright copper pennies to know what he said. She watched their eyes take it all in like kids at the carnival for the first time.

As they finished the tour and came back to the entrance, having dropped Angel and Sam off at their room, Ned said, "Now I don't want to be no blatherskite about this, but I just have to say, this is the most beautiful house I ever did see. Miss Caroline, this is the kinda place where you belong. And Mr. Adair, I'm so happy you're not the kind of feller to be toplofty about all this."

Caroline wished Angel were here with her pad and pencil. She leaned to Roderick. "I'll get the tea kettle on and get out the Christmas cookies while you take Ned and Fred out to the cottage."

Only a few moments passed before Angel joined Caroline in the kitchen. Caroline had pulled a dictionary from the shelf in the library. She handed Angel a slip of paper. "Hurry, Angel, before they get back. There's a dictionary on the counter. Look up these words I wrote down."

Angel sat down on the stool at the counter while Caroline plated the cookies. "Ned's still up to his learning a new word every day, and I can imagine he'll be practicing on this trip." She searched the dictionary. "Let's see. Apple-knocker refers to an ignorant or unsophisticated person. Hmmm." She turned several more pages. "Blatherskite is one who talks a lot without making sense." She thumbed on through the dictionary. "Where in the world does Ned come up with these words? For a minute, I thought he was learning self-descriptive words, being as he's not so sophisticated. But he's far from ignorant. He does talk a lot, but he seems to always make good sense." She ran her finger down the page. "Gamophobia . . . Well, this is it. Describes the Pendergrass brothers perfectly. It means 'fear of marriage or commitment.'"

Caroline turned around to the island as she broke out into laughter.

———•———

Roderick opened the door to his cottage and welcomed Ned and Fred. "I'm sorry there's only one bedroom in the cottage, but there's a day bed in my office where one of you can sleep comfortably, and there are two bathrooms. One's in the master suite, and the other's in my office."

"We'll be mighty fine right here, and it's all decorated up for Christmas too. But where you gonna be?"

"I'll be down in the tack room in the barn." Roderick reached for a small bag he had packed earlier. "Let me get this out of your way."

Fred nudged Ned, and Ned nodded in agreement. "You know Fred don't talk much, but I can tell you what he's thinkin'. We both thinkin' you ain't sleepin' in no barn while we're up here in the lap o' luxury. We'll be sleepin' in the barn."

"Not this trip. It's all taken care of. The tack room was my apartment until I built the cottage, and I'll be very comfortable there."

Ned shook his head in seeming resignation. "While we's alone, I want to say somethin'. Now Mr. Sam done tol' me about the anonymous package and the letter. Pure meanness. But you don't need to be worryin' about that on your weddin' day. That was the one thang that made Fred and me say yes to yer invitation. We're here to be on alert for any hinky person that wants to stop this weddin'."

Roderick smiled and extended his hand to Ned, realizing there was no purpose in discouraging him. "I appreciate that. I knew I could count on you, but I do want you to enjoy yourselves while you're at Rockwater. You're our special guests. And you'll be glad to know I've hired extra security. Now take a little time to get settled in, and then go back over to the house. Caroline's preparing us an afternoon treat."

Roderick's phone pinged. A text from Leo. *I'm parking at the barn. Meet me.* "Gentlemen, I'll be back up to the house in a few minutes. Need to get my bag out of your way and down to the tack room." He grabbed his duffle bag and left the cottage hurriedly.

Chapter 12

From Nothing to Something

———◆———

Wednesday afternoon, December 16
Rockwater

Leo was pacing when Roderick entered the tack room and threw his bag on the bed. "I'm assuming you have news."

"I wish I did. We've hit a brick wall. We have nothing."

"What about the fingerprints?"

Leo stopped pacing and looked at Roderick. "Received the box Sam overnighted early this morning. Checked the prints on the box and the pillow. No doubt the package and letter were delivered by the same person. Same fingerprints, and even some others. But none of them were in the system. I even called in some favors from some old buddies of mine from my FBI days. Nothing."

"And you have nothing else on Liz Bevins?"

"Like I told you before, she was in Richmond at the time they were delivered. No doubt about that. I even checked bank and credit-card records to see if there had been an unusual withdrawal or charge that might suggest she hired it done. Nothing."

Roderick walked to the window and looked out. "Outside of Liz, I haven't a clue who has any reason to do this. Makes no sense."

Leo unzipped his jacket and draped it on the chair at the small desk. "You're assuming it's somebody you know or some old flame who wants to get back at you."

"Well, don't you think that's a logical assumption? I have said goodbye to a few ladies, and I have made a few folks unhappy with some business decisions. It's all that makes sense."

"What about Caroline?"

Roderick turned away from the window to face Leo. "What's that supposed to mean?"

"Boss, have you asked her if she knows anyone who might not want her to leave Moss Point and marry you?"

"No. I've kept my conversations with her to a minimum about this. I don't want her worried or frightened."

"Then maybe it's time you talk to her. Does she have an old flame who might be the jealous type?"

"The only man in her life was David, and he died in a mudslide in Guatemala several years ago. She hasn't even dated since."

"Makes no sense. She's this beautiful, single woman living alone in a small town for nearly eight years and no fellows interested in her. You sure about that?"

"There's a professor at the University of Georgia who came on strong for a while last spring, but I think Caroline took care of that."

Leo pulled a note pad from his pocket. "Got a name?"

Roderick paused and closed his eyes. "Yeah. Spencer. Dr. Wyatt Spencer. Psychology professor. I thought his primary interest was Bella, but I know he was interested in Caroline."

"It's not much, but it's something. They're probably on Christmas break, and I won't be able to track down much. Even if it's this guy, Boss, I really don't think you should worry about it. My gut tells me this was amateur stuff. A psych professor would be no amateur. But I'll check it out."

"Good. Sooner than later. And let me know what you find out."

Leo picked up his jacket. "And I hope you're right about not bothering Caroline with this. I understand your reasoning. But she's an intelligent woman who knows I'm working on this, and she's bound to be curious as to what's going on. You might think about just telling her and assuring her that we have everything covered for the next few days. Nobody will be able to spoil your wedding day."

Roderick walked toward Leo and shook his hand. "Thanks, Leo. I appreciate all that you're doing. I know it's Christmas, and these extra guys are wanting time with their families."

"Yes, sir, but you're making it worth their while. There'll be lots more under a few Christmas trees because of you." He walked toward the door and turned around. "Now, you stop worrying. Relax. This is my job. Your job is to get married."

———•———

Caroline brought in a tray of cookies and six steaming mugs of hot chocolate. Roderick stoked the fire in the library and turned to Martha. "Mrs. Carlyle, you taught your daughter to be such a cordial hostess. Here she is the bride, the honored guest at a lovely dinner just an hour ago, and now she has on an apron."

"Lilah has a stash of aprons. Glad I found them."

Martha smiled. "She was the lovely belle of the ball this evening, and I'm glad to say she's always had a gracious heart. And smart she is, putting on an apron over that winter-white dress."

Caroline put the tray on the coffee table. "We could have changed clothes before we relaxed in front of the fire, but it's late, and I thought you might be tired. This hot chocolate will help you sleep." She passed the cookie tray and napkins and handed mugs to her parents and to Sam and Angel. Then she joined Roderick on the love seat and handed him his mug. "Sarah's the real hostess. She knows how to plan and host a wedding celebration."

"Yes, she does. She had a bit of help from Lilah, but she had the finest of teachers. Our mother was known for her skills at hosting parties."

Caroline's dad spoke. "Roderick, I so wish we'd had opportunity to know your parents and to thank them for raising such a fine son and daughter. And your friends? My, they are impressive, and every one of them had only wonderful things to say about you. I couldn't be happier that my daughter will be among such fine folks."

"Thank you. Many of them are longtime family friends who knew my parents and even a few who knew my grandparents. They've been in these parts a long time, and they're good people. I try to align myself in the business world with honorable men and women who see business as a means of making the world a better place. They may be bottling bourbon or raising horses, but they're doing it for good. You met the best of them this evening." He turned to Caroline. "And my Kentucky friends and business associates met the best of the best this evening too. Caroline, you were the most beautiful woman there." He leaned to kiss her cheek.

"Thank you, my love. I do look forward to getting better acquainted with some of them if they'll take me in."

Roderick chuckled. "Oh, my dear. Your problem has nothing to do with my friends taking you in. Your problem will be keeping up with your social calendar for the next few months. You'll be on everyone's lunch list."

Sam spoke as though he was pronouncing judgment in his court room. "Yes, sir. Our girl is like her mother and my Angel. They all know how to light up a room. You won't ever have to worry about Caroline embarrassing you. These women know how to be ladies in every circumstance, charming and disarming ladies, I might add."

Angel brushed Sam's arm with her napkin. "Stop talking like that. My cheeks will turn red. And speak of lighting up a room. I could see through the loggia windows that all the lights were out in the cottage except for the Christmas-tree lights in the window."

Sam piped in. "Yeah, those boys are sound asleep. I'm certain they were so excited about making this trip that they were up well before dawn this morning."

Roderick leaned forward. "I couldn't persuade them to go with us tonight. So, Lilah prepared them a meal, and they settled in early."

Angel asked, "Is there a television out there?"

Roderick responded. "Yes, a big screen."

"Then a team of horses couldn't have pulled them out of your cottage. They've never seen *Magnum P.I.* on a big screen." That brought a chuckle from everyone.

"Before we left, Lilah told me she was setting them up with a couple of Christmas movies and popcorn." Caroline turned to Roderick. "You know they may decide to move in."

The ring of a telephone interrupted their conversation. Finally, Sam said, "Angel, I think that's your phone again."

Angel grabbed her purse buried in the cushion next to

her. "Nobody calls me this late at night. Must be a wrong number." By the time she rummaged through her purse and found her phone, she had missed the call.

Caroline noticed the change in Angel's face after she looked at her phone. "Could be Santa checking up on you."

"I've already sent him my list." Angel turned to her husband. "Sam, it's late, and before I tarnish my sterling reputation of not embarrassing you, I think we'd better turn in." She stood. "Roderick, it's been a perfectly lovely day and evening. Being here to celebrate with you two and to celebrate Christmas is the best. And we have another beautiful day coming tomorrow. So, I'm saying good night."

Martha stood and extended her hand to J. "And I'm following Angel. We girls need our beauty sleep. Tomorrow will be like Christmas Eve around here with the rest of the family arriving. We'd better take advantage of a good rest tonight and a peaceful morning tomorrow. That may be the last of the quiet until after the wedding Saturday."

Caroline and Roderick rose for goodnight hugs. Roderick spoke. "I'm so glad you're here. I hope you all rest well, and I'll leave the hall lights on. We'll have the coffee ready at six thirty for those who rise early."

As their guests left, Caroline sat back down. "I think I'd like us to enjoy the fire for just a little while longer." She extended her left hand into the lamplight. "Roderick, I know I already said so, but the engagement ring is exquisite. I'm so glad to have it back on my finger."

"A rare pearl and setting for my rare gem. I was pleased that Mr. Harrigan was able to have it ready in time. I didn't want you to make it to the celebration party this evening without an engagement ring on your finger. I would never have heard the last of that from Sarah."

She nestled closer under his arm that was around her. "I do love the ring, but I'd rather have your arm around me than a ring on my finger." She looked at the ring again. "The rose gold is nothing like I've ever seen before. I'll never take it off again."

"Oh, maybe just long enough for me to slip your wedding band on that finger. Rings without end just like my love for you."

Caroline and Roderick were left alone in the library to savor the last moments of the evening and to go over the plans for Thursday. Images of Angel's face kept returning to Caroline's mind, but she said nothing of it to Roderick.

———•———

Angel stopped at the guest-suite door and turned to Martha. "It's been such a busy and beautiful day. Hope you get a sweet night of sleep before the crowd comes in tomorrow afternoon."

"This will be a Christmas gathering we won't soon forget, won't it?"

"It will be a Christmas to remember for sure." Angel and Sam stepped into their bedroom as J. and Martha climbed the stairs to their suite.

Sam removed his suit coat and draped it over the suit stand next to the bathroom door. "Well, you certainly know how to bring an abrupt halt to a cozy evening. Are you truly that tired?"

Angel took her phone and tossed her bag to the chaise lounge before she sat down in the straight chair at the writing desk. "No, I'm fine, but I truly couldn't wait any longer to call Gracie. She's called three times this evening, and the only message she left was to call her as soon as I could."

"I guess she thought if she called three times, you'd call

her sooner." He sat down on the foot of the bed. "Oh, she and that GiGi Nelson are probably still trying to worm their way into a wedding invitation. Those women just won't quit."

Angel put her elbows firmly on the desk and looked at her phone. "Nope. She knows that's not going to happen, but I suspect I know what this is about." She stopped talking and continued staring at the phone. She wasn't so certain now that she wanted to know what Gracie might tell her.

The sound of Sam's voice broke her trance. "Well, for someone so all-fired in a hurry to leave the company of some fine folks to talk to Gracie, you seem to have put the brakes on."

"Maybe it's too late to call her, and I'll just deal with this tomorrow."

Sam got up from the bed, walked to Angel, and put his hand on her shoulder. "All right. I've seen you play this Scarlett O'Hara scene a few times in the sixty years we've been married. So, what is it that you don't want to deal with right now because it will make you crazy, so you'll just deal with it tomorrow?"

"Hopefully nothing."

"Just hopefully? That means you know something. Might as well tell me now. Won't be any easier in the morning, and you won't sleep a wink tonight."

"You're right." She paused and looked up at Sam. "I baited Gracie."

"What do you mean you baited Gracie?"

"I told her about Caroline's package and the letter we got."

Sam backed up and sat down on the bed. "You did what? We were trying to keep a lid on this, and you told Gracie, the woman who talks to every woman in Moss Point at least once a week?"

Angel turned in her chair to face Sam. "That also means that she listens to every woman in town once a week. She swore to me she'd keep it under wraps, but if I know Gracie—and I do—she'll find a way to check things out. And if anyone in town can find out anything, she will."

"Well, what in tarnation are you waiting for? Call her."

Angel looked at her watch. "Sam, it's almost eleven o'clock. That's late to be calling someone."

"Gracie's up—she just called you a few minutes ago. I imagine she's pacing the floor with her phone in her hand, waiting for you to call just so she can tell you what she thinks she knows. You just don't want to know what that might be. Is that it?"

"Maybe. But what if she's got real information? What can we do about it?"

"You can bet your lacy white bonnet we'll do something about it."

"Sam, Martha and J. don't even know about this. All of this could blow up in our faces, and it's Christmas, and the wedding's two days away. We don't need to put a big stain on these celebrations."

"It's a bit late to worry about that. If we find out something, we'll tell Roderick and let him handle it. He'll know what to do, and he has security staff."

She put the phone down and clasped her hands together. "And what about Ned and Fred? I feel honor bound to tell them what we know if we find out something."

"Well, Fred doesn't speak, and Ned's not about to open his mouth about this. Just make the call, Angel. Then we'll figure out how to deal with it."

Angel picked up the phone and slowly punched in the numbers. The phone rang only once before she heard Gracie's voice. "Why haven't you called me? I've been dying to talk to you."

"I know. I'm sorry. It's the first time I've had a minute to call. We've been to a very lovely wedding celebration this evening and got home late."

"Well I have news, and you really need to hear this."

"Really?" Angel watched Sam pace at the foot of the bed.

She listened as Gracie told her all the details for the next five minutes.

"I can't believe it. And you're certain no one else knows "That's a shocker, but thanks for telling me." She imagined Gracie was grinning from ear to ear.

Gracie answered. "No, Angel, nobody else knows. I kept my word to you. But I thought you should know. Hope you sleep better tonight."

"Thank you, Gracie, and good night." Angel put the phone down and looked at Sam. "Sam, sit down."

Chapter 13

Confessions and the Castle

———————◆———————

Thursday, December 17
Rockwater

*B*efore the sun was up, Angel was dressed, makeup on, and hair refreshed. She rested on the chaise lounge and watched the clock. "Sam, you're slower than my IRS refund check. Come on. It's nearly six o'clock. I want to get to the kitchen and tell Caroline and Roderick the news before everyone is up."

Sam buttoned his sweater. "And what makes you think they're in the kitchen so early?"

"Roderick said the coffee would be ready by six thirty, and it won't percolate on its own. He and Caroline and Lilah are getting breakfast ready. I just feel it, so let's go. And besides, you know Martha. She may already be in the kitchen cracking eggs."

"Well, then, there's no hurry, is there?"

"I'm gone." Angel was out the door and down the hall. She heard laughter in the kitchen from the hallway. She was relieved to see only Caroline and Roderick. "I knew you'd be up."

Caroline was getting out the Christmas mugs but walked around the island, hugged Angel, and pulled out the barstool for her to sit. "Did you rest well?"

"Yes, thank you, better than I expected. No need pulling out the stool. I don't want to sit. I have news, and you need to listen in a hurry before your parents get in here. Can we go to the morning room in case they come in?"

Sam strolled into the kitchen and started to pull out a stool. "Good morning, good morning."

"Sam, don't sit down, and don't talk so loud. I need to tell Caroline and Roderick what we know."

Angel strutted hurriedly into the morning room, sat down at the breakfast table near the window, and started her story before they were even seated. "I'll get right to the point, and if there's time, I'll tell you the whole story. I had a call from Gracie last night. The mystery is solved, and we know who left the package for you, Caroline, and who left the letter in our mailbox."

Angel watched the astonishment on Roderick's face—either doubt that it was truly solved or doubt that Angel could have solved it. Roderick pulled out a chair for Caroline. She sat down slowly. "You know?"

"Yes, and you are in for a big surprise." Angel was just about to tell them when Martha's voice echoed through the kitchen.

"I came down to help with breakfast. I hear voices, so I know you're around here somewhere."

Angel could see the puzzled look on Caroline's face and the worried look on Roderick's. "You're not to worry about this. I'll tell you later."

Martha walked through the doorway and joined them. "There you are. I smell coffee and bacon, but I don't see any signs of biscuits and eggs."

Caroline rose and hugged her mother. "We're having maple-roasted bacon and pancakes this morning. The bacon's in the oven, and the batter for the pancakes is already made. Lilah's on her way, and we'll just heat the griddle and scramble the eggs when we're ready to serve breakfast."

The group chatted about plans and weather until Ned and Fred knocked on the kitchen door at exactly six thirty. In a matter of minutes, Caroline and Lilah, who'd arrived a little earlier, had a platter of pancakes and bacon on the breakfast table in the morning room, with the eggs following soon behind. Angel had kept everyone's coffee cup filled as they waited. They all sat down to a clatter of plates and silverware.

As the hearty meal came to a close, Ned wiped the last drop of maple syrup from the corner of his mouth. "Now, Mr. Adair, you will be one blessed man to have breakfast like this every morning. Why, even when we eat at Mabel's, we don't get nothin' like this."

Roderick smiled. "Well, Ned. I'm so glad you're here to enjoy this breakfast."

Unable to sit still and hold the news, Angel squirmed, crocheting buttonholes in the back of her chair cushion. She took the final bite of bacon and the last sip of coffee. "Would you please excuse me for just a few minutes?" Blaring her eyes and tilting her head, she looked at Caroline. She rose from her chair and tapped Caroline on the shoulder as she passed behind her.

Caroline rose quickly, following Angel's lead. "Are you okay? If you need the restroom, the nearest one is in the mudroom right off the kitchen."

With frustration, Angel said, "No, no, I don't need to use the bathroom, but I will if I don't get to tell the story. It was Jay Johnson. There's no need to worry anymore."

Noting Caroline's bemused expression, she told her what she knew and how she'd found out. "It's such good news, I think we should tell everybody and make a joke of it. What do you think?"

The color returned to Caroline's face, followed by giggles. "Oh, wow! Unbelievable. That boy . . . He's kept me on the fence for the last three years as to whether I should choke him or hug him. But I like your idea. Let's just make a funny story of it. That should diffuse the situation."

"Let's do, and I think you should tell it." After Caroline agreed, the two of them returned to their seats at the table.

Table conversation was slowing just a bit, and Angel looked at Caroline, raising her eyebrows. Realizing she should tell the story before Angel did so for her, Caroline turned to Roderick and spoke. "Roderick, you will learn that this family truly loves stories, and the more they are told, the more embellished they are. So I have one for everyone this morning." She smiled, "I just wanted you to know that you have a bit of competition, because . . . I have an admirer. A secret admirer who truly doesn't want me to marry you."

Roderick's wasn't the only face showing confusion. Angel couldn't help but grin as she looked at Sam in anticipation.

Caroline turned to her parents. "Mom and Dad, Roderick and Sam and Angel already know this, but last week I received an anonymous package warning me not to marry Roderick."

Martha gasped, and unable to contain herself, Angel picked up the story. "Yes, and Sam and I received an anonymous letter advising us to keep her from getting married. It gave us cause for a bit of concern since they were delivered directly to our doors. But the more we thought of it, the less sense it made." She felt Sam's hand on her arm. "It's okay, Sam. They all need to know, and I'm just telling them all at one time."

Caroline's dad leaned closer with his elbows on the table, a frown gathering on his face. "What kind of package, and exactly what did the letter say?"

Caroline told them about the heart-shaped red pillow cut in half with the stuffing falling out, accompanied by the warning that her heart would be broken like that if she married Roderick. "And basically, Sam and Angel's letter said the same thing, only it warned them to keep me from marrying him."

J.'s frown deepened, and Roderick interrupted. "You're not to worry about this, Mr. Carlyle. I have my security team on it. They are guarding Rockwater, and they are doing a thorough investigation."

Angel broke in again. "Well, I'm just going to bust a gut if I don't get to tell the rest of the story. You can call off the dogs, Roderick. It was Jay Johnson."

She watched Roderick nearly come out of his seat as both of his eyebrows moved toward his hairline. "Jay Johnson? I've heard that name before." He swiveled to Caroline. "Isn't that one of your talented students you've told me about?" She nodded, and he turned back to Angel. "Are you sure?"

Angel smiled broadly and relaxed. "Just as sure as I am that your Caroline will be the most beautiful bride Kentucky has ever seen."

Roderick sat back in his chair, his eyes thoughtful. Caroline placed her hand on his arm. "I know he's exceptionally smart, but he's only eleven."

"He's old enough to have a great big crush on you, and he's heartbroken you won't be his piano teacher anymore." Angel grinned with pleasure.

Roderick put his arm around Caroline. "But how do you know these things, Angel?"

"Two confessions. Mine first. You see, I told Gracie."

"And who is this Gracie?"

Angel giggled. "She is the owner of Cuttin' Loose, the only decent beauty shop in Moss Point. I sort of baited her because I figured if anybody would know something or could find it out, it would be Gracie. It seems Jay stole the pillow his grandmother was given after her open-heart surgery—the red one they always give to heart patients to hold on to when they cough. I have one of those myself, and I should have recognized it."

Caroline agreed. "You're right. That's exactly the pillow."

"Well, while she was getting her hair done, Jay's grandmother casually mentioned her missing pillow to Gracie. And Caroline, you know Maggie Johnson. I'm sure that pillow was proudly displayed on her living-room sofa so she could tell everyone who visited her where and when and how she got it. Well, when Gracie heard about the pillow, she put two and two together and called Jay's mother just to fish around a little bit. After Gracie's ten-minute conversation with her and another ten-minute conversation between Jay and his mother, there was a confession. Jay may be smart, but not smart enough to get rid of the evidence of the letters he typed on his dad's laptop."

Sam spoke up. "Oh, it gets better." He turned to Angel. "Let me tell this part."

Angel grinned. "Go ahead. This is your favorite part."

"Jay's got a wise dad. Mr. Johnson had Caleb, the sheriff, come to the house and give Jay a good talking to. Caleb told Jay he'd broken laws and that he could be prosecuted if Caroline wanted to press charges. That got Jay's attention, and I can only imagine the letter of apology you'll be receiving, Caroline. There'll probably be pages of begging you to forgive him."

Roderick laughed. "Press charges on a kid for having a super crush on Caroline? Then I'd be serving a life sentence, guilty as charged. I'm just so relieved. I need to call Leo and give him the good news." He stood, leaned over to Angel, and hugged her. "And you're right, Angel, we can call off the dogs and know that our Christmas celebration and this wedding will be perfect." He squeezed Caroline's shoulder and left the room with his phone in his hand.

———•———

The remaining morning hours passed quietly. Caroline noticed a few more gifts under the Christmas tree in the library as she added hers. She put in a call to Brother Andy and talked with Lilah to see if everything on their lists had checkmarks. Their work was done. All details were taken care of, and there was nothing left to do but enjoy these three days with the people she called family.

The afternoon hours were spent napping and preparing for their late-afternoon drive to the Castle to join the family for dinner. All day, whether with family or alone, Caroline sensed her emotions were barely held beneath the surface of her skin. Almost anything brought a tear—a sweet story from her dad, the sound of a familiar Christmas carol, remembering the sleigh ride here last Christmas, the afternoon light coming through the loggia window. Her heart was full.

Late in the afternoon, as the sky turned gray and the clouds hung low, they gathered in the library for a cup of hot cider before leaving for the Castle. Roderick announced, "Just talked to Chip. He's bringing the van around front. He thinks we should leave a few minutes early because it's beginning to snow. This drive is beautiful, and we want you to enjoy it while it's still light."

Caroline watched Roderick usher everyone out the front door, and she observed the way he assisted Angel, her mother, and Lilah into the passenger van. Again, her emotions bubbled, her heart brimming over with gratitude that she could be marrying a man who gave such attention to others, even to renting a van where they could all travel together. Just before a tear left her eye, she had to muffle her laughter as Ned and Fred climbed in, Fred whispering something in his twin's right ear again.

Chip took the driver's seat and turned the radio to a channel playing Christmas music. "To the Castle in Versailles?"

With everyone seated, Roderick took his seat next to Caroline. "Yes, indeed. To the Castle, and I'm glad you agreed to join us, Chip, especially since it has started to snow."

"I'm just grateful to be included, sir."

Ned was the first to speak. "We're going to a castle?"

"Oh, no, not *a* castle, to the Kentucky Castle. Sits on fifty-plus acres of prime Kentucky real estate. You'll think you've arrived in medieval Europe, but the food's better. Caroline's brothers and their families will be staying there overnight in the guest suites."

Caroline's mother added, "I spoke to James and Thomas a couple of hours ago, and everyone's there, settled in, and they've been exploring this afternoon. Betsy and Mason were just pulling in while we were on the phone."

Caroline pinched Roderick's arm. "And Sarah and George, Roderick's sister and her husband, and Gretchen and Bella will there."

Ned said, "Well, that just beats a hog a-flyin'. We gonna see Miss Gretchen and Miss Bella and eat at a castle. Nobody's gonna believe this when we get home, Fred."

Roderick chuckled. "We'll send you pictures so you can prove it. We'll put you two in one of the four turrets and take your photo. I talked to Caroline about getting married there, but she chose Rockwater."

"Yes, sir, and I know why. I ain't never seen nothin' so beauty-ful as Rockwater."

Caroline smiled to herself. "I agree with you, Ned."

The drive to the Castle was magical. After a few moments, silence replaced their chatter. Large snowflakes drifted and found places to rest on the loblolly pine boughs and limbs of white fir trees lining the roads. Caroline lamented to herself that it would be dark before they returned to Rockwater, and she would be forced to wait until morning to see the blanket of snow over the rolling hills of her new heart's home. She softly began to sing along with the choir on the radio—"It Came Upon a Midnight Clear." Only her mother and Lilah joined her. The rest continued their ride in silence.

They arrived at the Castle, greeted the family, and dined like royalty. And around the table, they shared not only good food but stories from their lives. Betsy, James, and Thomas told Caroline stories. Sarah and George told the funny Roderick stories, and Lilah told the sweet ones. They all laughed loudly, and a time or two Caroline saw her mother, Angel, Lilah, and Gretchen silently dab at their eyes with a tissue. Caroline observed Ned and Fred sitting side by side, never saying a word, and Gretchen and beautiful Bella next to them. She just wanted to take it all in and file away every detail so that she could recall the memory every Christmas and anniversary.

Roderick stunned her by retelling the story of her kidnapping in Guatemala, and how he feared he had lost her forever. He vowed again never to allow anything like that to happen to her. She watched Gretchen and Bella as Roderick told the story, and she could hear Bella softly humming. Gretchen didn't even try to quieten her. It was the song that Bella and little Rosita, the Mayan child, had shared two thousand miles apart while Caroline lay injured in the Guatemalan jungle. It was the perfect backdrop to Roderick's story. Reliving the experience was less painful now and more beautiful because Rosita would adopted by George and Sarah. Caroline glanced at Sarah. They exchanged knowing smiles.

Before the evening came to a close, Caroline made the rounds to everyone, pinching Thomas's ear for telling the story of how she tried to pay for the air the gas station attendant put in her tires. Mason got the familiar raised eyebrow for some of his comments, but Caroline cared not about a few embarrassing moments. Her heart was full, knowing the people she loved most in the world were all in the same room, celebrating life, family, Christmas, and her wedding.

As the hour grew late, they rose from the table. Betsy and Josefina walked hand in hand with Caroline through the castle lobby. Josefina stopped. "CC, did you bring me candy kisses like you promised?"

Caroline reached inside her purse and pulled out a red satin bag. "Now, what do you think? I always bring you candy kisses. This is enough to last you until New Year's Day, but always ask your mommy first." Caroline knelt to kiss Josefina but held her just for a moment to look at her, her caramel skin, her brown eyes, her dark hair falling in curls to her shoulders, and a tiara leaning to the left. "Josefina, you are the most beautiful little princess I have ever, ever seen. I love your red dress and the sparkly tiara you're wearing." She looked up and winked at Betsy. "Your mommy told me that's all you wanted for Christmas: a tiara. I'm glad your grandmother gave it to you so you could wear it while you're here at the Castle. I think she'd enjoy getting a photo of you dressed up like this. But she'll get to see you all dressed up on Saturday. Your grandparents will be here for the wedding. And I'll be showing those photos to little Rosita. I can't wait for you to meet her. Just like you, she's from Guatemala, and she's coming to live with Sarah and George. I think the two of you will be great friends."

Caroline felt Josefina's chubby little arms go around her neck, and then she heard her whisper, "And we can both visit you at Rockwater or maybe the Castle. I like being a princess more than anything, CC, but I can only be the princess one more day. Mommy says I can't be the princess the day after that because you're going to be the princess. CC, I hope you like being the princess as much as I do. Do you want to borrow my tiara?"

Caroline could hardly contain her tears. After years of grieving and feeling like the life had been squeezed from her, her once barren spirit now teemed with joy and vibrant hope and, most of all, love. She whispered back to Josefina, "Thank you, but I think you should wear it to the wedding. And you know, I think I'll like being a princess just as much as you do."

Chapter 14

Christmas Surprises

———— ◆ ————

Friday, December 18
Rockwater

Caroline rose early on Friday morning. Today's excitement stole her sleep. Food preparation. Practice with Bella. Wedding rehearsal run-through. And an evening full of family Christmas celebration.

Opening the curtains of the window, she looked out on fresh white snow blanketing the hills as far as she could see, the pine boughs drooping with the accumulation. She hoped the icy temperatures would keep the flakes on the pine needles from melting in the glistening sun. A white Christmas and wedding. All her family would be here for most of the day, and they'd celebrate a family Christmas at Rockwater this evening. And tomorrow, they'd be joined by remaining family and friends for their wedding. This day seemed like a fairy tale, but it was real. The eve of their wedding.

Caroline walked to the writing desk, sat down, and turned on the lamp. A sleepless night had turned into a productive one of recording her thoughts and writing cards late into the night, and she wanted to reread them this morning. Each note had to be penned perfectly, for they were expressions of her love and gratitude to family members and close friends and to her new family members. She picked up a card. Printed at the top was *Caroline Carlyle Adair*. These notes would be her first communication as Mrs. Roderick Adair. She read each one and stuffed it into its envelope and sealed it before scripting the name of its recipient on the front. Her plan was to choose moments during the reception to hand these notes to the people she cherished.

Then there was the final card, the note to Roderick. She would arrange with Lilah to place it on his pillow in the tack room tonight as a surprise.

She looked at the clock. Ten minutes before seven. She checked her hair and makeup and stepped into the hall. There was her mother at the top of the stairs.

"Good morning. Wait, and I'll join you." Caroline took her hand as they walked down the stairs together.

Martha smiled. "I guess this is my opportunity to walk you down these stairs. Tomorrow it will be your dad's turn. You did say you were entering from the stairs, right?"

"Yes, that's right."

"And you'd best remember there'll be no one up here except your dad to help you with your dress. So you two must be careful as you make this turn on the landing. We'd like a grand entrance, but with both of you on your feet."

"Mom, tell me this is really real, that I'm not just fanta-sizing. I've dreamed of this day for the last ten months, but it's too perfect to be real."

Martha stopped at the bottom of the stairs. "It is real, my lovely daughter. Roderick's love for you, your new home, your hopeful future. It's all so very real, and I couldn't be happier for you. Sometimes I wish you weren't so far away, but your dad and I won't be around forever, and I'm so grateful you're happy and not alone. That's what's important to us."

"You may be seeing more of me now than ever. I'll have time on my hands."

Her mother chuckled. "And Roderick has a plane and a pilot, right?"

Caroline's eyes widened. "You must be wrong. This can't be real."

As they walked toward the kitchen, Martha asked, "Remind me. What's on today's agenda? I know you're having a brief wedding rehearsal just before lunch."

"Wish I could get by without that, but I think it will make everyone feel more at ease. At least we're all here and it'll be casual. I can promise you it won't be like any other wedding rehearsal. I've seen so many of those turn into fiascoes. Everything will be simple. I just need to show the wedding party members where to stand and talk through the ceremony."

"Oh, and don't forget Josefina."

"Yes, Josefina. She's so excited. And Bella will play. Chip's going to the Castle early to pick her and Gretchen up so I can go over things with Bella before the others arrive. I still don't know how much she understands about what's happening, but she plays so beautifully. There was no one else I wanted to play." Caroline led her mother to the piano, and they stopped briefly to look out the windows at the snow-covered courtyard.

Martha ran her hand over the raised lid of the piano. "Are you sure Bella's ready?" she asked as they walked down the hall.

"Yes, ma'am. A year ago, I wouldn't have been so sure. I wouldn't have known what she might have decided to play and when she might play it. But I'm certain. She'll rehearse with the group at eleven. If I have any doubt, I'll move to Plan B, my recording."

Her mother stopped in the kitchen doorway and looked at Caroline. "You? You have a Plan B?" She laughed out loud. "Miss Caroline Careful herself. I should worry very little when it comes to you. You've had a Plan B since you were three."

Lilah closed the oven door and turned to face them. "Biscuits in the oven. So, what is all this funny business going on between the two of you this morning?"

Caroline grinned. "We're were just talking about my Plan B for the wedding music. Mom's not certain that Bella won't come out with something surprising, maybe like Johnny Cash's old song 'Flushed from the Bathroom of Your Heart.'"

Caroline enjoyed seeing Lilah double over in laughter. "Ooh, child. I'm with your mother. Surely Bella wouldn't do that, and surely Johnny Cash never sang that song."

Martha raised her right hand as though taking an oath. "I promise he did. You can ask Thomas. He sang it in a talent show when he was a junior in high school, and Caroline accompanied him."

Lilah handed Martha an apron. "So glad you folks bring such fun and joy, and I'm going to love having you all around here. Now take this apron so you don't mess up that lovely Christmas sweater, Martha. I could use your help."

———•———

Caroline opened the front door to Gretchen and Bella at nine fifteen. Bella hugged her and hurriedly headed to the piano. Caroline took Gretchen's arm and followed Bella. "I wonder which piano she'll choose." She squeezed Gretchen's arm as they watched. "I knew it. She chose my Hazelton Brothers piano. But she'll have her own grand next week. You two sleep okay in the Castle?"

"Like we'd been sprinkled with Castle fairy dust."

"I'm so glad. I can imagine that you were having thoughts of your homeland. You've probably seen real castles, some hundreds of years old."

"Oh, yes, I have climbed the hills to see the castles that line the shoreline of the Danube River near where I lived. And to see them at Christmastime was magical. I cannot explain it, but lately, I have grown homesick for my homeland. Thoughts of taking Karina and Bella with me to Austria in the spring make my heart so happy and give me so much to look forward to. I want so much to find my sister, Elfi. The day I took the money and my grand-mammá's hand mirror and ran away with no hope of ever returning, I had no chance to tell her goodbye. I only hope to see her again."

"We will find her."

Gretchen stopped and turned to Caroline and took both her hands. "In my heart, I still am amazed you and Roderick will go with me."

"Yes, and we will do some research before we go, and maybe we can find your parents too."

Caroline noticed the slight turn of Gretchen's head and her steady gaze through the loggia windows as she spoke as though she'd gone far away. "I dare not think that I could find my parents alive. I have accepted that life has been difficult for them and they have already left this world. I can only hope to find Elfi." She looked again into Caroline's eyes. "But let us not speak of this today. Let us take joy in every moment that we all have here together."

"Let's do." Caroline dropped Gretchen's hand. "Mom

and Lilah are in the kitchen, and Lilah has a tea box filled with your favorite teas. Would you go and make certain to let me know quickly if Roderick appears? He took all the guys to town after breakfast and said he would be back in time for rehearsal. I prefer that he doesn't hear any of the music Bella and I will be making."

"I will make certain he hears not a note." Gretchen headed toward the kitchen.

Caroline sat down next to Bella on the piano bench and went through the music. Caroline had wisely made a recording of all the wedding music in the exact order it was to be played. Bella, the rare musical savant whose brain and musicality were unexplainable outside her being a true gift, would play exactly what she heard, and Caroline knew it.

Bella played with perfection, and Caroline practiced nodding her head for the next selection. Bella played on cue, never faltering or hesitating. When they were almost done, she asked Bella to play the wedding song she had written for Roderick, and she sang it softly. She wondered if she could do it or if she should stick to the recording she had made.

Eleven o'clock brought the rest of the family and Betsy and her tribe. Lilah greeted them at the front door and took those not in the wedding party out to the morning room and entertained them while Caroline did what she'd done probably two hundred times in her role as a musician. But this time was different. It was her wedding. The rehearsal was simple and short. Caroline was pleased.

At eleven thirty as planned, Lilah brought the rest of the crowd into the loggia around the piano. Martha stood from where she had been seated to observe the rehearsal and joined her husband. Caroline saw her dad look at his watch as he took her mother's hand.

Then J. spoke. "Well, I think we all know what to do, and we're looking forward to doing it. The way I figure, in about twenty-four hours, Martha and I will have a new son, for the two of you will have said 'I do.' With your permission, Roderick, I'd like to have a prayer of blessing for us all as we celebrate the birth of our Lord Jesus this evening, and as we celebrate your wedding tomorrow."

Caroline felt her tears coming.

Roderick spoke, "I'd be humbled and grateful for that, Mr. Carlyle."

Lilah added, "And I'd be grateful if you could also thank our good Lord for the lunch that has been prepared for us all too."

When J.'s amen was said, with Lilah's instruction, the crowd moved toward the dining room where lunch was served buffet style. "Enjoy the light lunch. Just fix your plates and eat wherever you'd like. Tonight, we'll serve a traditional Christmas dinner, and we'll all be seated around the table."

After lunch, the afternoon provided time for them all to either relax by the fire in the library or to play in the snow. Caroline and Roderick took her brothers and their wives and Betsy and Mason and the children on a sleigh ride up to the edge of the forest for sled rides down the hill.

Time seemed suspended at the top of the hill as Caroline watched James and Thomas and Roderick playing with the children and sledding down the hill. She noted how Roderick paid close attention to Bella and rode with her on her sled. She, Betsy, and her sisters-in-law made snowballs for the snowball fights. Caroline was experiencing sheer joy, coming from a deep place of gratitude. There was no doubt that their decision to be married at Rockwater was the right one, a place where it would be a true family affair—one they would all remember.

The sky grew darker, and large snowflakes began to fall as the day faded into late afternoon. Everyone was back inside and enjoying the fire when the doorbell rang. Roderick excused himself to answer the door.

When he returned with a guest, there was no hiding Caroline's surprise and joy.

"I heard there was a rocking Rockwater Christmas party tonight and a wedding here tomorrow. I'm here to crash it." There was Dr. Lydia Pipkin, standing next to Roderick and almost a head taller, carrying a large Christmas bag. She was dressed in jeans and a heavy sweater with a brown leather jacket and a wide-brimmed leather hat.

Although they had spoken by phone, Caroline had not seen Lydia since their return from Guatemala in July. She rushed to embrace her. "You did come."

"Of course I did." Dr. Pipkin kissed Caroline's forehead.

"But I thought you were in Africa with the children's choir and couldn't get back for Christmas."

"Had a change of plans. Got to thinking about how we almost lost you in Guatemala and how your brothers and Roderick came to rescue us. I couldn't miss all this. Might as well get used to it. I'm family now—I saved your life. And besides, I could imagine Thomas walking around barefooted in this cold weather without his shoes. Remember? I wore them home from Guatemala. So glad he had big feet."

Caroline had told her family and Sam and Angel about Dr. Pipkin and the story about Thomas's shoes. She heard him laughing louder than all the rest.

"Come here. I'm returning your shoes." Dr. Pipkin handed him a large Christmas bag.

Caroline looked at Roderick. "You're just a Jack-in-the-box of surprises, and this one is the best one yet. I had no idea."

Sam stood up and spoke. "Well, this seems a lot like Christmas to me. That very first Christmas was a big surprise too. God Himself coming to earth. We had no idea what we needed and what would make us complete and joyful, but God did."

A loud "Amen" resounded around the room.

———•———

After a Christmas dinner around the dining table, Roderick led them all back into the library for their Christmas gift exchange. There wasn't an empty chair, something for which Roderick apologized. "When you come back next Christmas, we'll have some additional chairs in this room."

The children and a few adults sat on the carpeted floor while they sang Christmas carols, told funny things that had happened with their families at Christmas, and Caroline told sweet stories from their last Christmas here at Rockwater. Roderick looked across the room at his sister, Sarah, snuggled next to George, laughing heartily with the rest of them. He caught her eye and nodded and winked. They both knew from now on Rockwater would be full of life and love and music, just like their mother would have wanted. There was Caroline now and little Rosita coming to join their family.

He got up, walked across the room, and pulled out a Santa hat from behind the Christmas tree. "We need someone to be Santa and pass out all these gifts. Do I have a . . .?"

Before anyone could respond, Dr. Pipkin was on her feet, removing her own hat and taking the Santa hat from him. "Since I'll be missing this opportunity with all my orphan children in Africa this year, I'd like to do the honors, if I may."

It was only minutes before the room lay knee deep in wrapping paper and ribbons, and oohs and ahhs reverberated as lids were lifted from gift boxes.

When the floor under the tree was bare of gifts except for the few reserved for Christmas Day, Roderick walked to the writing desk and took the large, leather-bound Bible and handed it to Sam. "It seems to me we're making some new family traditions—Mother Martha's fruitcake for our dessert just like last year, and Sam, it would be so meaningful if you'd repeat your reading of the Christmas story from the second chapter of Luke for us."

Sam took the Bible and opened it and began to read in his King James voice.

Roderick surveyed the faces of those in the room while Sam read, so grateful for these people whose lives were now entwined with his. He and Sarah truly had family again. When Sam finished, Caroline led them in singing "Silent Night."

The house was quiet again after most of them left to return to the Castle. But Roderick knew they would return tomorrow for even a happier day—the day Caroline would become his wife.

After Lilah left, and everyone else had gone to bed, Roderick and Caroline returned to the library for a few stolen moments alone. He loved how she so naturally curled up next to him on the sofa. He played with her hair that fell just beneath her shoulders and spoke softly. "It's been a long but wonderful day. In fact, I don't think I could imagine a more perfect day—you, your family, my family, Dr. Pipkin, new traditions, and snow."

Caroline turned and looked up at him. "Yes, I fear you've royally spoiled me with two white Christmases. I'll be expecting a repeat every year."

"I'll do my best. I told your father you were God's precious gift to me, and I promised him I'd protect you, make you smile every day, and provide you with the freedom to do and be whatever puts joy in your heart. And if it's snow at Christmas, then I'll get a snow machine if necessary."

"I was right. I am royally spoiled." She stretched to kiss his stubbly cheek.

"Well, then, I might as well give you an early wedding present to add to the spoiling." Roderick pulled a tiny box from his shirt pocket underneath his sweater and placed it in her hands.

With a curious glance at him, Caroline carefully unwrapped the box and lifted the lid. She removed the contents and twirled it between her fingers. "A heart-shaped key? The key to your heart, maybe?"

"Oh, my sweet, you've had the key to my heart since the first time I saw you. It's an antique heart-shaped key. Now come with me, and let's see what it opens." He took her hand and led her down the hallway to the master bedroom and opened the door. They entered, and he closed the door. "Now to the en suite." She followed him into the massive closet. He pointed to the island in the middle of the closet. On one end were five drawers, each about five inches high and the width of the entire island. Each drawer had a lock. "Try the key."

Caroline approached the end of the island and inserted the key into the top drawer. The key turned easily, and she pulled the drawer open slowly.

He watched her face as she first saw the sparkling jewels filling the black velvet-lined drawer. He observed as she ran her fingers across the ruby necklace and earrings before looking up at him. "Roderick, this . . . What? I don't know what to say, but this is too much for me."

He took her hand. "I beg to differ with you. It's not nearly enough, and all you have to say is that you will wear my mother's jewelry."

"This was your mother's?"

"Yes, and her mother's and both her grandmothers'. That's why there are five drawers of jewelry. Sarah and I divided all of it years ago, and she prayed I would be married one day. This is all yours now, my wedding gift to you. I know that jewelry is not necessarily important to you, but I hope you will treasure these pieces. And perhaps one day you will give them to our children. Why don't you open the rest?"

Roderick watched the surprise and disbelief wash through her eyes with the opening of each drawer. He knew she was overwhelmed, and he cherished that about her. "These pieces have been locked away in the bank for years. But they're home now because you're here. Lilah took everything down to Mr. Harrigan to have it all cleaned and polished, and then she placed it all here for you."

"I'm so sorry. I just don't know what to say, other than I'm very grateful. And I will wear these pieces, and I will treasure them because they belonged to your mother, the wonderful woman who gave birth to you, my love. And I look forward to the day we can pass them on to our children. But we have so much living to do before then."

He embraced her. "That's all you need to say," he whispered in her ear. "There's one more little thing." He pointed to the antique wooden chest atop the island. "This is my never-worn-before wedding gift to you, and I assumed I'd not be allowed to see you in the morning."

"That's right. Not until I come down the stairs on my dad's arm. But I won't open this gift until you open this one." She reached into her pocket and pulled out a small box and placed it in Roderick's hand.

He opened it and remembered seeing the jade cufflinks when he picked up her things in Guatemala that unforgettable, painful night when he thought he might never see her again. "I've seen these, and they are handsome cufflinks."

"And when did you see them?"

"In Guatemala when I was searching your bags in the hotel looking for anything that might help me find you."

She stepped nearer to him. "They're made from the finest Guatemalan silver and the rare blue jade prized by kings and princes."

"Thank you, my love. I'll wear them tomorrow. They'll always remind me of the morning I found you in the jungle, the blue morpho butterflies flying around you as though they were keeping you alive just for me." He kissed her gently and then pointed to the chest. "Your turn."

She opened the chest to find a single strand of pink pearls and pink pearl earrings, each topped with one small pink diamond. She picked up the strand and held it in the light. "Oh, my goodness, they're exquisite, Roderick, just like my ring."

"That's what Mr. Harrigan said when he found them. Will you wear them tomorrow?"

"Tomorrow and every day after that." She laid the pearls down, and her arms encircled his neck. "Roderick, you do know I would love you just as much without all this, don't you?"

"I do know that, and it makes me love you more, if that's possible." He held her close. "Merry Christmas Wedding, my love. Let's lock up. You need some rest, and I need to get to the tack room. I have a few things to do because we're getting married tomorrow."

Chapter 15

Wedding Song

———◆———

Saturday, December 19
Wedding Day at Rockwater

*I*n her last few minutes alone with Bella's last piano prelude in the background, Caroline looked at herself in the mirror in the remake of her mother's simple white gown, now off the shoulder, softly draped and trimmed in delicate lace, flesh-pink pearls encircling her neck, and her loose curls atop her head thanks to Betsy. No veil and no princess tiara. She gazed at the wedding bouquet she held tightly in both hands –white linen handkerchiefs, fluffed and arranged among the white roses and maidenhair fern. But there in the middle was the surprise—Roderick's monogrammed handkerchief nestled around one single white iris blossom. He always remembered.

The sound of bells brought her back to this moment in time.

Weeks ago when she'd learned that Gretchen rang handbells as a child, she persuaded her to ring Christmas wedding bells to announce the wedding hour, and now the shimmering sounds echoed through the halls of Rockwater. Eleven o'clock. Caroline knew Bella would start to play the piano any second now, and her father would be knocking on the door. Sixty family members and invited friends were in their seats in the loggia for the ceremony. Her last thoughts before opening the bedroom door were prayerful thanks for how God had led her to Roderick and asking His blessing on all that would take place today.

When Caroline opened the door, just as she expected, her father was waiting. He kissed her cheek, extended his arm, and said, "You may become a married woman today, but you'll always be my daughter, and a beautiful one you are."

Holding fast to her tears of sheer joy, she took a deep breath, and said, "Thank you, and thank you for being the kind of man who showed me what marriage can be. I love you, Daddy."

They walked gently down the hallway balcony to the stairs. Her life seemed to play like a fast-forward movie as she peered into the loggia filled with people she loved. Seeing Bella at the piano and waiting for the last echoes of bells to fade, she focused again as she made the turn to the stairs. And there, in front of the two-story windows overlooking the dressed-in-white hills of Rockwater, stood Roderick, handsome, smiling, and looking up at her as she approached the stairs. She remembered the cautious words of her mother and made the turn slowly and adjusted her gown before descending.

Bella began the bridal march just as planned. Step by careful step Caroline and her father made their way down the last flight of stairs and through the aisle created by the placement of chairs. She smiled at the thought of little Josefina showering the marble floor with the white rose petals she now walked upon. When they reached where her mother was seated, she paused long enough to take her mother's hand and whisper, "I want you to walk with us the rest of the way."

With her parents beside her as they had been all her life, she finally, finally reached Roderick. She felt the squeeze of her father's strong hand before he placed her own into Roderick's waiting palm. She sensed the movement of her parents taking their places behind her. But more than that, the warmth in her chest reminded her of all that was in front of her. Just as Brother Andy began, she felt the tug on her arm and looked down to Josefina's smiling face.

Josefina whispered, "Here, CC, I saved you some." Caroline quietly chuckled at the rumpled white rose petals in Josefina's open hand. As soon as Caroline took them, Josefina grabbed the tiara atop her head and handed it to Caroline. This time she didn't whisper so politely. "You can wear it, CC. You're the princess today."

Caroline heard the wave of soft laughter ripple across the room. She took the tiara, knelt, and put it back on Josefina's head, kissed her cheek and whispered, "But you're always the princess. Today I'm the queen." It made Josefina laugh.

She rose and took Roderick's hand again as Brother Andy spoke, claiming the moment. "Well, we have a little bit of a crown adjustment going on up here. If this weren't such a beautiful wedding ceremony, I'd launch into a sermon because I've just seen the picture-perfect sermon illustration, maybe one appropriate even for a wedding. After all, marriage is a union where two people give up their pride and agree to humbly, yet fiercely, love and serve each other without either of them wearing a crown."

After the Scripture was read, comments made, the vows promised, and the rings exchanged, Brother Andy invited them to kneel on the prayer bench for the final prayer. Just as he closed his prayer without the amen, as planned, Caroline winked at Bella. Bella began to play. Still kneeling, Caroline turned to Roderick and began to sing—no recording, just music and her voice from the deepest part of her being. She swallowed her tears and kept singing as Roderick's tears dampened his face. She had never felt such love. Pure love. Her voice soared.

Forever love, love forever,
Love will light our way.
Eternal love from the Gift and the Giver—Love eternal, we
*   pray.*
*   One starry night in Bethlehem, moonlight hovered a*
*   manger.*
*   On bed of hay in swaddling clothes, to the earth a*
*   stranger*
*   Came the One who would save us and give us forever.*
Forever love, love forever,
Love will light our way.
Eternal love from the Gift and the Giver—Love eternal, we
*   pray.*
*   One starry night in coldest December, moonlight on*
*   snow drifts*
*   Lighting hearts and paths of two whose love was a gift*
*   From the One who would guide them and give them*
*   forever.*
Moon and stars or bright blue sky, rain clouds or rainbows,
Heart to heart, hand in hand, in joy or in sorrows
*   Forever love for all our tomorrows.*

Forever love, love forever,
Love will light our way.

Phyllis Clark Nichols

*Eternal love from the Gift and the Giver—Love
eternal, we pray.*
Love forever, we pray. Amen. Amen. Amen.

Caroline sang her Christmas wedding song as the perfect benediction to their sacred and intimate ceremony. She felt Roderick's gentle and yet strong grip as he helped her stand from the kneeling bench. There was holy silence until Brother Andy asked them to face their friends and introduced them as Mr. and Mrs. John Robert Adair III. Bells rang again, and Bella played as Caroline and Roderick passed through the aisle, facing all their applauding and smiling family and friends.

The hallways and dining room were soon filled with their guests as they helped themselves to the buffet. For the next two hours, the halls of Rockwater resonated with remembrances and laughter and well-wishing and even a few Merry Christmases. She and Roderick made a point to speak to every guest, and Caroline delivered her handwritten notes to her parents, her brothers, Sam and Angel, Sarah and George, Gretchen and Bella, the wedding party, and Lilah. She particularly took joy in placing her note in the hands of Ned and Fred, dressed in probably the only suits they had ever owned, hair slicked down to their scalps, and grins on their leathered faces.

At exactly one thirty, just as Roderick had prepared her, he gave the final toast, expressed their gratitude, and explained he and Caroline would be at the front door to speak to everyone before departing. Guests began to leave, and an hour later only Caroline's parents, Sam and Angel, and Ned and Fred were standing at the door in travel clothes with their bags in hand. Acer and Chip began hauling bags to the van for the trip to the airport.

Caroline's mother asked, "Are you sure you don't need

us to help clean up?"

Roderick answered quickly, "That's very kind of you, but it's all taken care of. The caterers and their staff finished and left fifteen minutes ago."

"Then I will tell you again what a perfect day it has been and how we couldn't be happier for the two of you." Embraces and tender words brought tears to all their eyes. Caroline noticed how her father took charge, allowing no more lingering, and ushered them all to the van with the warning that they must get home before Christmas. Caroline felt Roderick's arm slip round her waist as they stood in the doorway and waved their goodbyes. When the van made the turn at the curve, Roderick closed the door.

Caroline turned to him just as he said, "Finally. We are married. We are home at Rockwater, and we are finally alone." Their arms encircled each other like the wedding rings on their fingers.

———•———

Friday, December 25
Late afternoon at Rockwater

"Caroline, Caroline! Where are you? We must hurry." Roderick called eagerly.

Her arms went around him from behind as he stood at the sink, and she spoke softly. "I'm right here, my love, and you don't need to yell." She felt him turn to face her. "And besides, I thought that's why you had this fancy intercom system, so that we can communicate with our gentle voices." She stood on her tiptoes to kiss his cheek.

"Sorry, I'm just a bit anxious about something before it gets dark. Where's your coat? I know where it is. I'll get it." He stepped away into the mudroom just off the kitchen.

"Oh, and I made hot chocolate for both of us."

"What are you talking about? We just got home from this whirlwind trip to see my family and Sam and Angel, all within forty-eight hours. It's Christmas afternoon, and we're home. I'm totally confused. We must be going somewhere if I need my coat. And you made hot chocolate?"

"I'll tell you on the way." He shoved her coat into her arms as he put on his heavy parka. "Put your gloves on too. Get your hot chocolate. I'll get mine, and let's go."

Caroline sensed his urgency. "Are you okay? You're barking orders, and I've never seen you quite like this."

He opened the kitchen door to the courtyard and motioned for her. "Sorry, it'll all make sense in a few minutes, but we must go now."

When she stepped through the door behind him, she saw the sleigh, the same one they'd taken a ride in last Christmas under a Kentucky full moon. "We're taking a sleigh ride now?"

He took her mug of hot chocolate. "Yes, right now. Climb in, please." He handed her both mugs when she was seated, took his seat, and wrapped a thick wool horse blanket over their legs. "One more Christmas surprise."

As they rode, her tension melted away like a dusting of snow on a sunny morning. "I'm not sure I can handle any more surprises. I've lost count."

"Oh, you'll love this one! And it will keep on surprising you. Sorry I couldn't produce a full moon this evening. That's why we must go now. These rolling hills get very dark when the sun goes down."

For several minutes, they rode in silence across acres of snow-covered grassland dotted with naked hardwood trees and pines. He stopped at the top of a hill that overlooked a meadow surrounded by a stand of leafless tulip trees. The sun was slipping fleetingly behind the trees along the horizon off in the distance. He dropped the reins, turned to her, and took his mug of hot chocolate. "This, my love, is your Christmas present."

"This is a memorable surprise—a sleigh ride to remember our moonlit ride last Christmas. A perfect Christmas present, and the perfect ending to our Christmas Day."

"No, this is your present." Her eyes followed his arm as he gestured across the vista. "This meadow is your present. You can't see it clearly from here, but there is a small pond with a garden bench underneath the tulip trees. And when you sit there in the spring, you'll be surrounded by irises. My mother loved daffodils and tulips, and we have acres of those. But last fall, I had Chip plant irises in this meadow just for you. Merry Christmas, and may this bring you years of pleasure being surrounded by your favorite blossoms."

"Roderick, there are no words. I'm so moved and so grateful, and I can hardly wait for springtime." Her gloved hand reached for his. "You make me feel like the most loved woman walking around on this planet."

"Only because you are." She felt the squeeze of his hand as she looked into his eyes. "The bulbs were planted in October, but they'll be up in late March, according to Fletcher. Now I know you like white best, but he planted every imaginable color, and to think that they will multiply through the years until this whole meadow is filled with them. We'll sit among them under the yellow blooms of the tulip trees, and this will be our garden where we'll spend many quiet sunsets."

"Nothing would make me happier than being here at home with you every afternoon for the rest of our lives." She kissed him and put her head on his shoulder. "My heart has been at home with you since I met you. And now, both our hearts are at home with each other here at Rockwater." She closed her eyes and breathed deeply. "We've both known loss and pain, and yet here we are holding on to the most beautiful love I could ever have imagined."

"I think our pain has taught us the value of moments, every moment, and I couldn't be more grateful for every moment with you, Caroline."

"And I with you, my love."

Wrapped in a blanket together, they lingered in the quiet of a Christmas sunset for several moments. Caroline's soulful humming interrupted the silence and gave way to softly sung words, words she sang to Roderick and to the Gift and the Giver.

Moon and stars or bright blue sky, rain clouds or rainbows,
   Heart to heart, hand in hand, in joy or in sorrows
   Forever love for all our tomorrows.

Forever love, love forever,
   Love will light our way.
   Eternal love from the Gift and the Giver—Love
      eternal, we pray.
   Love forever, we pray. Amen. Amen. Amen.

About the Author

Phyllis Clark Nichols's character-driven Southern Fiction explores profound human questions using the imagined residents of small town communities you just know you've visited before. With a strong faith and love for nature, art, music, and ordinary people, she tells redemptive tales of loss and recovery, estrangement and connection, longing and fulfillment ... often through surprisingly serendipitous events.

Phyllis grew up in the deep shade of magnolia trees in South Georgia. Born during a hurricane, she is no stranger to the winds of change. In addition to her life as a novelist, Phyllis is a seminary graduate, pianist, soloist, and cofounder of a national cable network with health and disability-related programming. Regardless of the role she's playing, Phyllis brings creativity and compelling storytelling.

She performs half-hour musical monologues that express her faith, joy, and thoughts about life—all with the homespun humor and gentility of a true Southern woman.

Phyllis currently serves on a number of nonprofit boards. She lives in the Texas Hill Country with her portrait artist, theologian husband.

Website: PhyllisClarkNichols.com
Facebook: facebook.com/Phyllis Clark Nichols
Twitter: twitter.com/PhyllisCNichols

Made in the USA
Columbia, SC
11 July 2021

41698436R00095